CLOSE TO THE FIRE

Close to the Fire

A Novella by
DAVID HELWIG

GOOSE LANE

Published by Goose Lane Editions with the assistance of the Canada Council, the Department of Canadian Heritage, and the New Brunswick Department of Economic Development, Tourism and Culture, 1999.

Edited by Laurel Boone.
Cover illustration ©Judi Pennanen, 1998. Reproduced with permission of the Artist.
Cover and book design by Julie Scriver.
Printed in Canada by Friesens.
10 9 8 7 6 5 4 3 2 1

Canadian Cataloguing in Publication Data
Helwig, David, 1938-
   Close to the fire
   ISBN 0-86492-272-8

I. Title.
PR9199.3.H445C56 1999   C813'.54   C98-950278-3
PS8515.E4C56 1999

Goose Lane Editions
469 King Street
Fredericton, New Brunswick
CANADA   E3B 1E5

for Judy
after all these years

I spake unto the Dutchess, and she said, "You wouldn't dare."

"Dutchess . . ."

"No," she said.

Back to staring at the fire, the tongues of yellow flame reaching up from the bright red embers of the logs as I stroked my little beard, and neither of us broke the silence. However, the Dutchess knows me for what I am. Recalcitrant is a word she has used, a word among many. Pig-headed. Two words among many. The Dutchess knows me for what I am, since what I am has been her fellow for years now. Ever since. Yes, ever since. So, knowing me for what I am, the Dutchess knows that I will do as I please. She will state, or even more likely overstate, her opinion, and I, when the fit is on me, will ignore it. That is what we were both thinking as we sat in comfortable chairs, the doors of the airtight open so we could see the flames, a cold rain falling outside, wind howling in the chimney. Gather round, children, gather close to the hearth, and wicked uncle will tell you things, such things. Tell us what? Of girls born out of their time, a face like Leonardo's "Girl with an Ermine," body by Cranach perhaps, the tiny waist and florid curve of arse below. In fact, I had forgotten about her since I saw her in the Registry Office yesterday, but the sweet thought of wickedness brought her back. Most lawyers send a clerk or a title searcher to the Registry Office, but I go myself. The phone never rings there. You hear a quiet bustle of pages turning and pencils scratching, and you save the money paid to the clerk or title searcher. Yesterday I was rewarded for my industry by the sight of this exotic thing, a face and body from another time, something from old paintings in old books, and wicked uncle looked upon her with the eyes of desire. I told the Dutchess about her, the Dutchess being tolerant of wicked uncle's eye. Without it she would not be here, would not be the Dutchess, would have another name altogether.

I have been reading, secretly. Grewgious defines true love. Chapter Eleven. Hush, the Dutchess will hear your thoughts. She stirred in her chair, knowing, and I quickly turned my mind to something innocent, the swelling behind of the Renaissance Girl, and the Dutchess was still again. It is the nature of wicked uncles to feel such stirrings of fancy, and the Dutchess ignores them. She was wicked enough once. Is still, perhaps. Tonight, I can tell, she will leave me limp and panting and sated, and she feels she has nothing to fear from my concupiscence, whereas what I had just proposed to her was a trespass.

No Trespassing. Trespassers Will Be Prosecuted To The Full Extent Of The Law. I did that once, prosecuted a trespasser, who just happened to be the brother of a previous wife of the trespassed upon, and somehow the case got laughed out of court. Not the only time. It is a good thing I don't take the law too seriously. It has a certain baroque splendour from time to time, and I enjoy the ingenuity of legal argument, have some bent for it, this verbal logic run wild, but mostly the process of law is a matter of bullying, conniving, and the not quite illicit use of influence. Still, every process must be lubricated somehow. Note to self: look up meaning of *lubricious*.

There can be no coolness, no lassitude, no doubt, no indifference, no half fire and half smoke state of mind in a real lover. Grewgious again. The Dutchess stirred and I stood and left the fire, made my way to the kitchen window and observed how the wind and the rain beat on those tall sentinels, the sunflowers. They would soon be killed by frost and stand like dead soldiers of some vanished war. *Dark intangible presentiments of evil.* The wind shook the flowers and the rain poured down, and the chill sent me back to the fire where the Dutchess sat straight in her chair, an old-fashioned college clipboard on her knees as she studied the flames and now and then made a note. She was at work on another article, prelude to an edition.

"The cheaper sort of red herrings are always too salt," she said, reading to me from one of her old books. I made an agreeing noise. Red herrings, yes, yes, of course. In the last few years, the Dutchess has come into her own, her studies of the history of domestic life just sharp enough to please a feminist audience while curious enough in their detail to intrigue the rest. At first I was dismayed at her success — it was bright eyes and smooth skin and lubricious afternoons that I had bargained for. One evening, as I sat at the large antique desk in my office, irritable and lonely (the Dutchess away at a conference on the Invention of the Mangle or some such thing), I wrote a title, *The Boy Who Got Everything Wrong*, and after the title I began to tell the little children one of wicked uncle's stories. After a secret pursuit of some months, I was able to announce to the Dutchess that I had written a story for children and that it would appear. When she read the book, she said I had stolen the whole thing from her anecdotes about a hopeless little gaffer she had met earlier in her professional life, when she was doing gigs as a substitute teacher. Very sniffy she was, and she told me not to steal from her again, and I claimed it was all invented from my own rich imagination, and we didn't speak for three days. Ever since she has been ready for war on the subject. Note: *lubricious*, also *lubricous* and (archaic) *lubric*, means just what wicked uncle thought it meant.

Autumn. It is the time of year for it. *A fire shines out upon the fast-darkening scene, involving in shadow the pendent masses of ivy and creeper covering the building's front. As the deep Cathedral-bell strikes the hour, a ripple of wind goes through these at their distance, like a ripple of the solemn sound . . .* I could hear from the other room the Dutchess bubbling like a boiling pot, aware of my thoughts, my trespass on her territory, but there was no stopping the thing now. I would ride it into the winter, and she would perhaps retaliate, and on we would go. The sunflowers held up their heads under the cold rain, the Dutchess made notes, and the wood in the stove burned. The season moved on; the colour of the leaves had begun to change, showing flashes of red on the rolling hills. A fox crossed the road on dainty feet. The Dutchess does not forgive, but she lets things pass and gets on with what must be.

The wind outside was loud and the rain beat against the window of the little back room where I sat on a straight chair, shivering but not unhappy to be there in the dark. The night was full of voices. This was once the Doctor's House, and these small rooms at the back, probably built for servants, now served as a home for shelves of books never consulted and occasionally as guest rooms if both the little Dutchesses arrived at once with children in tow. The little Dutchesses are Orland's daughters. After they were born and before I met her, the Dutchess had been fixed, although she was still a young woman.

Here, once upon a time, servants lay still in their beds, muddled girls who hoped to find a farmer or fisherman as tall and straight as the sunflowers. One stood outside the door, listening. The doctor dreamed of new refinements of disease. Rooms away, the Dutchess was snoring quietly. I had lain awake for a while, and then I had got out of bed without disturbing her and wandered down the hall to the small back rooms where one might wait for ghosts to come. Orland collected ghosts. His book was on the shelf near where I sat. Orland was a good bit older than the Dutchess, but she and I are of an age.

It was when the world was young and I breathing my few months of Irish air that the Dutchess was born of respectable Dutch parents in the Netherlands and named Marijke Van Zuylen. At the time the family emigrated, she was three years old. I had come ashore a couple of years earlier. When I first learned all this, I started to call her Dutch, which evolved to Dutchess.

She calls herself Mary Van Zuylen these days, but at the time I met her, she was Meg Fothergill, so renamed in and by marriage to Orland Fothergill, famous folklorist and cuckold. She was also called — by me but not out loud — the Dairy Queen. Young Meg, child bride (though already mother of two), had perfect creamy skin, breasts that watched serenely from low cut dresses; she gave the wonderful impression of being made of the finest quality dairy products. All butter and eggs. And I so lean and hungry. The Dutchess has blossomed a little since, developed an aristocratic scope, and I have kept in step.

Just how miffed would she be if I went ahead? It had been a long wait since my one thin book, and now this idea had arrived, prompted by what she told me about her work (as had the last — I'd have to admit that). Well then, she was an inspiration. Why was she so possessive? Did she have to keep it all to herself? I could have ideas, too, with a little stirring about. The further history of that evil man John Jasper was much to my taste. Let the wicked uncle enquire into the possibilities of his wickedness. *I love you . . . I would pursue you to the death.* There had been a time when I was determined to make the Dutchess leave her husband, but she wished to stay, and I had pursued her to the death. The wind shook the window and told old stories. She had no right to prevent me.

Farewell, my sweet, I'm on my way. The morning was foggy, and in the dim early light, only the few trees close to the road were visible. Beyond, hills and the salt sea. Two large crows rose from the side of the highway where they had found roadkill to feed upon, and they flew blackly off into the mist. *Oh Billy Magee Magar.* Orland taught me that song about crows pecking the eye of a dead horse, same tune as all those other fierce songs, the folk not having a wide range but a good ear for a note or two. Orland teaching old songs and his wife waving her milky things.

The Dutchess teaches Life Skills three days a week, but this wasn't one of her days. On her teaching days, we sometimes drive the long road to town together, but this morning I had left her all loose and soft in a pink dressing gown, surrounded by Victorian recipes, the bag of flour ready to be thrown all over self and kitchen. Not a tidy cook, the Dutchess; we are not a tidy pair, things fall into disorder about us. Deep in her researches, she produced more food than even two well-grown adults could eat, and I found myself taking this and that — Lardy Cakes, Devonshire Splits, Corn Chowder, Lancashire Hot Pot, Skirlie, Leek Pie — off to town to be distributed.

Another crow in the mist. *Oh Billy Magee Magar.* Note to self: try to find the words for the song. A truck with Nova Scotia plates raced past, in a hurry to be somewhere. Life Skills. How to go out for milk. Reading the label on the aspirin bottle before feeding them all to the baby. How to write a cheque, but not if you don't have a bank account. She does a brisk business with criminals, the thought being that if they knew how to get along better they would stop their criminal behaviour. Judging by criminals I have represented in court, this might have something to it, for they are, most of them, tediously foolish and fucked up. Defending these people is always tricky; they don't like you telling the court they're stupid. Often Dwayne or Kevin Thief will have ideas about his own defence, and a good deal of time is spent explaining that he shouldn't say he was far off in another city, since a constable grabbed him ten minutes after the theft, two blocks away, with the loot in his possession. Send him to the Dutchess to learn Life Skills.

More crows in more mist. *Oh Billy Magee Magar.* A few days back, the Dutchess came upon a farmer cutting cabbages and got a box of them at a good price, and we spent last night cutting them up and laying them down in a crock for sauerkraut. And yesterday afternoon, stirred by the sight of machines in the fields, I took my yearly look at Sir Charles God Damn sonneteering in 1886 on the potato harvest. *A clamour of crows that fly in from the wide flats where the spent tides mourn.* Same crows fly still over the fields. *Oh Billy Magee Magar.* Now downhill to the bridge over the river, line of cars, fog thickens, cormorants on the abutments, birds of ill omen, murderous sailors out there invisible in their dories, the oars splashing as they come toward you to do you to death. The old seas were full of wooden ships instead of debris. *In memory of HECTOR CAMPBELL Master Mariner who was lost with all his crew whilst in command of the ship Aeternia of St. John N.B. on a voyage from Rangoon to Liverpool in Nov. 1872 Aged 33 years.* The Dutchess found that in the graveyard up the road. She is fond of death, the Dutchess is, reminded by it that she is so largely and voluminously alive and has years of trouble yet to make for me. Now and then I wondered if she had always, always, always been faithful, if she didn't just once find a lad whose need for Life Skills included warming between the white cheeks of his instructor. She had deceived Orland so easily, but then he was older and suffered from one of those tedious things, what do they call them? Dysfunctions. He could breed but not please, and the Dairy Queen, in all her creamy whiteness, insisted on being pleased. I (she being permanently plugged) could please but not breed.

Into the city, a church spire appearing out of the fog. Dickensian. Fateful word. The wicked uncle would, must, evoke the wicked uncle. Later in the day I would go to the university library and look at some things. The Dutchess had arranged her schedule so that she gave her weekly class there — History 387, as adjunct lecturer — in the morning of one of her Life Skills days. They continued to have her, but as money grew ever tighter, there would be more pressure to send her away. Who was interested in the History of Domestic Life when it was possible to study Computer Science and Entrepreneurial Development? Life Skills, Parts 2 and 3. Still, her course was part of Women's Studies, and that was still a good racket. *There were three crows sat on a tree, oh Billy Magee Magar.* I parked the car and stopped on the way to the office to buy a package of cigars for Elaine, my secretary. It was her birthday, and I was one of the few who knew of her secret vice.

I spake unto the Dutchess, and here is what I said.

"Wouldn't it be a grand thing, Dutchess, if your chap was known as the Man Who Finished *Edwin Drood*?"

"You wouldn't dare."

"Dutchess . . ."

"No," said the Dutchess.

Chaps do not encroach on the territory. Rule One.

How is the territory to be delimited? Question One apropos Rule One.

In the course of her rummagings a while back, the Dutchess came upon a book called *What Shall We Have For Dinner? Satisfactorily Answered by Numerous Bills of Fare for from Two to Eighteen Persons*, a Victorian curiosity published as the work of Lady Maria Clutterbuck. We discovered it in a bookstore in Moncton while we were on our way back from Montreal. Just her line of country, of course, made more piquant by the fact that Lady Maria Clutterbuck was in fact Catherine Dickens, wife of the Inimitable, as he liked, grandiloquently but fairly enough — there was no other like him, God knows — to call himself. She has been looking into Dickens while doing an article on the book and planning to do a new edition of it. By the rules of East and West Dutchessville, that means that I should keep my hands off him. I will admit that the idea of the unfinished novel came to mind because the Dutchess left various biographies of the Inimitable lying around, and, doing a little rummaging of my own, I was reminded that Dickens had died in the midst of darkish Drood. I discovered that the book had been finished by others, yet the thing gnawed, nagged, picked at my eyes, and so, on a cool and rainy afternoon as we sat by the fire, the picture of domestic bliss, I got up my courage and spoke. John Jasper, wicked uncle, demanded it of me.

A play, I thought. Time to go back to the theatre

perhaps. The theatre is where I had met the Dutchess, far off in Upper Canada, when she was quiet, blue-eyed Meg. Butter wouldn't melt in her mouth, I thought, though there were rumours. I was a student at law and bored senseless. When I saw an advertisement, auditions for *The School for Scandal*, I went along. I had displayed myself in high school and once or twice as an undergraduate, to notable effect I always thought, and my lovely mother thought so too. I fancied myself as the hypocrite Joseph Surface and was nonplussed all to hell to find myself cast as his honest brother, Charles. The hero. I never wanted to be the hero but was set to it by the hand of Fate, old busybody, old pimp, and I found myself playing scenes with a demure young woman, modest as could be, who, I was astonished to learn, was married and the mother of children. Though she seldom spoke except to read her lines, she looked at me from time to time, and her eyes were so very blue that I looked back and looked back. I met her ancient husband (younger then than I am now) who was good and true and adoring. When the little imp playing Sir Peter hinted that she could be had, I was immensely displeased. That he might know, or think he knew. By then, I was in a lather about her. I wanted to be with her in the paradise garden. The night she first appeared in costume, her white breasts scandalously, sumptuously, maddeningly on display in a naughty eighteenth-century décolletage, I felt a bit dizzy and thought I might faint. Just as we were about to make an entrance that night, she turned to me, plumped up her titties and said, "Don't you think I should be playing Lady Teazle?" Lady Teazle, who'll tease and perhaps do a good deal more, the misbehaving wife of an older husband. Two lines into the rehearsal of the scene I dried, and no amount of prompting would bring the lines back. Later, offstage, passing through the dark wings of the little theatre toward the dressing rooms, she so close in front of me, I put my hand on her bare shoulder, and she stopped, and I drew her to me, put my arm around her neck and pressed my hardening thing against her sweet Dutch arse and bent to kiss her skin. She gave a soft sigh, and that night we consummated the affair behind a bush in a back lane.

I am touched still by the memory of how she began to come to my little apartment up a flight of stairs in a grey stone house, but the question is, when did she begin to have firm opinions, when did Rule One come into effect, and Rule Two and so on? I approve, on the whole and of necessity. Dairymaids must grow up and become Dutchesses, who cause a very different brand of trouble, but I can't perfectly tell just when it happened. I suppose she always got her own way. She had decided to have me, I am told, and did, got herself into my bed in spite of the difficulties of family life, but I was meant to be a passing fancy and refused to pass. Perhaps the flood of tears when she got on the train with me, leaving Orland and the little Dutchesses behind, washed away some kind of innocence.

A play about the Drood case. Would that bring it all back? We have escaped. We are two settled bodies somewhere *nel mezzo del cammin di nostra vita*, and neither much wants to venture into any dark woods nor trail about the underworld following ghosts, not even the wiser ones. Besides, Drood has been made into a Broadway musical. Still it lies there, always unfinished, as provoking in its way as was the sweet young arse of Orland's wife.

"No," said the Dutchess. "No, no, no."

Late afternoon, and wicked uncle sat in the chair behind his office desk and looked out the back window at the rare autumn sunlight on a brick wall, light the rich colour of a fine pilsener in a tall glass, falling into an alley where cats were known to roam.

> *Down in the street cries the cat's meat man,*
> *Fango dango with his barrow and can.*

One of the comic ditties that the Inimitable performed with his sister, when his father was trotting him about showing everyone that the little bugger was smart as a tick, stood up on tables to perform, clever boy, clever boy, and learned that he was somehow to be famous. Like the little Mozart, though without the same divine skills. Still, brother and sister performing together, it all comes out in the wash. Wicked uncle was paging through two volumes of biography when he should have been dealing with a zoning dispute as described in the file on his table. Swot up details, then go to see the town clerk to enquire what can be done to allow said restaurant to build said deck in said alley, tastefully screened from what went on round about. Tomorrow. I am on good terms with the town clerk most of the time but mustn't be seen to push. The actual zoning bylaw and appended survey not perhaps relevant but must be committed to memory. In the outer office, Elaine is scanning something we have on CD ROM that might be of use, but we both know that what will be of most use is flattery: tickling the clerk who will tickle the council.

The days grow short, the sunlight precious to us here in the north end of the continent. In a bit, wicked uncle is meeting the Dutchess for a meal, and I am very tempted to drink more than my share of the wine and eat to excess and later to sit by the fire sipping Jameson's and bring on bad dreams anent the lost body of Edwin Drood. Murder most foul, a delicious thing.

Of course we don't know that he has been murdered, not for certain, though young Charley Dickens says he asked and was told. Poor dead Drood, poor dead Ed. And John Jasper, wicked uncle, a black figure in deep mourning, leaning on the sundial waiting for the girl who is frightened of him, of his menace and adoration, who shrinks from his touch even as he claims her, claims even her anger and scorn. Delicious. Perhaps it should be a movie. Narrated in the third person by an educated, musical voice At the end, we see a man in a cell, and as the camera moves in, we are aware that he is speaking, and that the voice is that same one we have been listening to, that the story we have been told is his own.

The door opened, and Elaine came in and caught wicked uncle staring out into Cat's Alley at the last of the late sun.

"Jane the Carpenter phoned," Elaine said. "When you were at the Registry Office."

Elaine doesn't like Jane the Carpenter and disapproves of our friendship with her, jealous because Jane comes to the house, although Elaine has been invited to the house and has declined. Elaine is, in her spirit, a creature of the marshes, at ease only among the dank places and foul vapours. She reads a lot of magazines — always a sign of rancour and disappointment. Though she is efficient and polite to clients, her belief that life has failed her goes deep. This dates from her husband's absconding with a cocktail waitress. It was then she taught herself to smoke cigars.

"Have you ever read a book called *The Mystery of Edwin Drood*, Elaine?"

"I don't read books," she said. "You know that. Except romances."

"You like those?"

"No, not especially, but they pass the time."

"And magazines."

"If my stupid reading habits are all we have to talk about, can I go home?"

"What will you do when you get home?"

"Mother's coming for dinner."

"What will you feed her?"

"TV dinners. It's all she'll eat."

"And then you settle back with brandy and a good cigar."

"She doesn't drink, and I don't smoke when she's there."

"I'll see you in the morning Elaine."

Note to self: look up those old pictures to see if the girl in the registry office really does look like them. Don't faces change from generation to generation? Or is the change in what we choose to see?

Come close to the fire, children, and wicked uncle will remember things from oh so long ago. Jackdaws, Harlech, being left in the rain, hiking along the road. All of that and more. It was today's crows started it, at their business of scavenging in the cold morning, the crows leading me on to the rooks of Cloisterham, and those leading to the jackdaws on the broken stones of Harlech castle, black birds, grey ruins, and in the distance the grey sea.

When Meg and I ran away, that was where we went, to England and then to North Wales. Once she had decided to go, she wanted to go very far, spent a little legacy from a grandmother to get us there. There was a plan, if only in my mind, that we might get as far as Belfast, my birthplace, but we never did, a result of poverty, grief, and the inability to stop screwing long enough to make a plan. We were scared of what we had done, of what might come of it, and half strangers to each other, but in the darkness there was no place for thought.

I looked out the window and saw the reflection of fire on the glass, our seasonal burning, wood fires as the days get shorter. In the cities, where I grew up, the steam pipes heat the malls and office buildings and apartments, heat by numbers. I turned away from the coming night full of other worlds, wandering planets, and I stared into the flame of the wood fire and tried to remember what it was we fought about at Harlech, standing in the ruins of the ancient castle, looking over the field of sheep toward the sea, but I can't, and I won't go out to the kitchen to ask the Dutchess as she stands on a floor covered with debris making a milk punch from the Clutterbuck book. Her cheeks will be a little red from working over the heat of the stove, her face intent. I can't bring myself to enquire what we broke our hearts about that day. She walked away from me as I stood by the grey castle wall, and when I turned to look for her among the ruins, there was no one. The grey day dissolved into rain. I waited for a bit, and then I went back to where we had left a rented car, expecting to find her sitting in it, perhaps still angry. It was gone. For the last two days I had been driving, wrong side of the road, wrong side of the car, always in danger of sideswiping an oncoming lorry or a stone wall. She had never once taken the wheel or wanted to, and now she had driven away. I was as bare as the stone and as old, frightened in an empty place, unable for a moment even to be angry but as absolutely alone as a man dying. I walked back into the castle and looked down the hill at the dirty-coloured sheep grazing in the rain, and I couldn't tell whether the wetness on my face was rain or tears.

I walked into the town, rain wetting my hair and clothes, and saw the car in front of a stone cottage.

Thinking she must be in there, I knocked, and a short woman with bright red cheeks, rivers of broken veins, an apron over a housedress, looked at me and said in her beautiful Welsh lilt, "Oh yes, your wife has said you would be along," and when I was in the house, she told me which room and that tea would be ready in a few minutes. Meg was waiting for me in the bed, her back to me, and she said nothing as I undressed and climbed in and lay behind her, never seeing her face until we were done. By then it was dark, and we went down the stairs for fried eggs and bread and butter and strong tea in front of a coal fire.

I put another log in the stove, and as I sat down in the rocking chair, the Dutchess came in with mugs of punch. Settled in her place, she took up a book.

"It does sometimes happen," she read aloud, "that when you are living in the country, in the neighbourhood of considerate gentlefolks who possess game preserves, that they now and then make presents of a hare and a few rabbits to the poor cottagers in their vicinity."

"No one has ever brought us a rabbit," I said. I warmed my hands around the cup of hot spicy punch. Dickensian punch on this dark and droodly afternoon.

Late at night, a celebratory glass of Jameson's in hand, wicked uncle stood by the back window and looked out across the lawn to the patch of overgrown woodland behind, celebrating another day of living, another night, the brightness of the moonlight on the lawn and on the leaves, leaves which were now beginning to fall. The owners of the property behind live far away. When we came here, the owner was an old woman somewhere in New Jersey, but she died, her nephews have inherited, and they are letting the house fall down and the land grow up in weeds and brush and trees. The apple trees have been untended and unpruned for generations. They produce small, bitter, pulpy apples that catch the light on sunny fall days, a parody of harvest.

We came to this house loaded with debt, half frozen between the futile wheezing of the old furnace and the gaping holes to the outdoors. I knew nothing about country life, how to chop wood or build walls. Trapped in a crawl space trying to insulate, my face covered with mud, panting with fear, I knew I would never survive. The trees in the woods behind were black and dead, covered with moss and lichen, drowned in brush, and at the edge of the lawn an old shed looked as if it might contain bones of murder victims, tools of torture, the impedimenta of witchcraft. It stands there still. Though the house is beautiful now, and warm, and the Dutchess has made gardens and lawns, we have never touched the shed. It is built across the property line, and some superstition has kept me from tearing it down or even hiring someone to tear it down. Just once in a brave moment of that first month — the house a ruin, too old, too broken, and we too poor — I went into the shed, and there I saw the remains of other lives. Such things. A basket full of the heads of dolls. Broken dishes. An inexplicable piece of fur that might have been the skin of a dead cat. Old iron and tin, three windows with broken glass. An enamel chamberpot with a rusted hole in the bottom. I looked quickly and went away, closed the door behind me, left the place to the spiders and mice and skunks. Do so still, the grey rotting wood a reminder of the cold days when some dark thing waited in the woods to take our heads, when we were still trying to learn to be together, in hell and paradise once an hour, organizing the little Dutchesses to come for part of the summer, counting the change in our pockets.

I stare into the world painted with moonlight, looking for the answer to the mystery of how to finish the unfinished. If I were writing another book for children, it would be simple. Wicked uncle would smile mysteriously upon the boy hero, and suddenly everything would change. Time would fold, and the two of them would be sitting in a Victorian drawing room, heavy drapes, much furniture softly upholstered, a coal fire burning, fog outside, and a bright-eyed figure with curly brown hair would burst into the room and begin doing imitations. There he would be, Dickens himself, and the young hero would contrive to ask him just what he meant to do about Drood and be entertained by his mime of the imp Deputy stoning Durdles home through the drunken night.

By the time of Drood, of course, he wasn't a bright-eyed creature but a man prematurely aged, deep wrinkles, one lame foot, priming himself with oysters and champagne in order to get up in front of the audience and kill Nancy one more time, and if he were to appear in front of me, I would have nothing to say except to warn him that he was exhausting himself. During his last appearances in London, on the first night he read the Sikes and Nancy scenes, his pulse went from 80 to 112, and on the second night to 118. His body was giving out.

We cannot have ghosts for the wishing, though wicked uncle invoke them with Jameson's. The Dutchess lay loose and white and happy in our bed, and wicked uncle stumbled about the cold house with a glass of whiskey in his hand and a black tuque on his head for warmth, seeking visions when he ought to sleep and dream. I turned from the moonlit lawn and the old shed to one of the bookshelves Jane the Carpenter had built. I found Orland's book of ghost stories and opened it, not knowing what I was looking for. Orland's name had come up in conversation twice recently, and I was suspicious. I read a few lines about horses that would not cross a bridge, knowing, as horses do, that an evil creature lurked on or near it, and as I read the lines, I was shocked to hear them in Orland's voice, as if he might be beside me reading aloud. Not the ghost I wanted, no ghost at all, for Orland was alive back there somewhere. The girls visited him, and he and the Dutchess wrote letters. I didn't know what they said, didn't wish to know, it would make the small hairs bristle. Monsters. The other people. Best keep them on television where they belong.

These thoughts stoned me home to bed, the glass left half full on a table behind me, lights out, time for sweet oblivion, dreams.

"Where were you?" the Dutchess said as I climbed back into bed.

"Looking for ghosts."

"Danger of finding them," she mumbled sleepily.

"Know it too well."

She rolled over and cuddled herself against me, all hot and soft.

"Orland," I said. "It was Orland's ghost."

"Yes," she said, "I suppose so."
Then, instantly, she was asleep.

Fire burning, rain falling.

THE MYSTERY OF EDWIN DROOD COMPLETE.
*Part the Second. 'By the Spirit Pen of Charles Dickens, through
a Medium.' Published in Brattleborough, Vermont, U.S.A. 1873.*

Dickens comes back from the dead, as Drood, perhaps,
came back from the dead to confront his murderer.
The medium sits up late at night in a dark room with
a single candle, listening to the wind, waiting, saying
magic words, until at last the pen begins to move on
its own and the Inimitable gives dictation, sitting in
the other world with his toasted cheese, laughing and
crying at the antics of his own creations. Inventions in
the mind of a ghost. How far from where I am, seeing
the green of winter wheat on the reseeded potato
fields, the black silhouettes of ducks and geese moving
across the sky, a bull standing in a paddock in the
autumn rain. The Dutchess is silent these days, and I
suspect her of plotting something.

At the university library I found an old book on
Drood, 1912, dated from Bay Tree Lodge, Hampstead.
All those English houses with their cozy names. Note
to self: get a sign, Wicked Uncle's Lodge, formerly the
Doctor's House. Everyone would take it for a bed and

breakfast. I learned from the old book that there were a number of Drood plays, one of them, never produced, by Charles Dickens the Younger with someone named Joseph Hatton. Charles Dickens the Younger. Wicked Uncle the Younger, no such critter. Come, my son, and I will tell you the story of my long and happy life, and you can tell it to the little ones.

Fire burning, rain falling. It was Donald Gillis who got us here. There we were in London, in a small residential hotel in South Ken, eating an English breakfast, porridge, boiled egg and two rashers, nearly out of money, making it last, no idea where we would go, I with a law degree of sorts, the Dutchess — but I didn't call her that, not yet — with nothing. Sometimes I thought that after the holiday was over, she would return home to Orland, who would forgive, and it would be a tall story to tell someday on the other side of the moon. Sitting over breakfast, I saw the keen eye of a long man with grey hair and a grey, considering face watching the pretty Dutch girl sip her tea. I knew he watched her as I had, helpless, stricken, and I was afraid that she would notice and run away with him.

Not quite what happened. I never had the illusion that Donald had any interest in me or my obvious cleverness. It was the lovely skin and bright eyes he adored. That's what made him set out to save us. The next morning he was at breakfast again, and he engaged us in conversation — we were Canadian, he was Canadian — and that day we went together to the British Museum, which we had missed, incompetent travellers always. There among the plunder of the ages our stories got told, and he affected to find ours romantic, and I was invited to return to Canada to become his junior, to be called to the bar here. He fell in love with the Dairy Queen, frightened for a girl who had fallen into the arms of a lustful lout without the brains to support her. That's how he saw me then. True enough, maybe. I proved competent at the practice of law, and I let him educate me. Though I was from away, as his junior I was accepted as having my wits about me, and I learned to interpret the quack and croon and chortle of the local accent.

I have thought sometimes that my lover loved another. They shared an interest in history, and Donald lent her books and insisted that she complete the degree she had abandoned to marry Orland. He was a kind man, perhaps even a wise one, and I, callow and hungry, couldn't be like that. I would say bitter things under my breath as I drove past the wet red fields of spring, the white hills of winter overlooked by the dark spruce. And then he grew thinner and greyer and died, and I took over the practice, paying something to his wife over the years.

Now we have been here forever. I have lunch with

Fred the stockbroker and Mike the government man, and I hear what the boys in the back room are saying. I know all the current lies and how to listen to them retold. I am worldly in a small way. I know which cabinet minister is on the booze and who can be bought and sold. I know people, meet people. I know a man, a retired policeman, who is preparing a landing field for UFOs. Today I stood in a government office and looked down into the street and suddenly, for a moment, eternally loved a pretty, anonymous young woman going by, swinging her way along through the autumn sun in a pale dress, a slit in the skirt showing the movement of her young and shapely legs. I watched from above, through glass, and knew we have one life each, that this was heaven, then turned and began to negotiate with the environment people on behalf of a client with effluent problems.

The book on Drood tells me that the mysterious figure of Datchery, the white haired "old buffer" who comes to Cloisterham and begins secretly investigating the probable murder must be Helena Landless in disguise, Helena Landless, *an unusually handsome lithe girl . . . very dark and very rich in colour . . . almost of the gipsy type.* Imagine the dark, lithe girl dressing herself in a man's clothing, undressing secretly by candlelight in her little bedroom near the old cathedral. *A white-haired person with black eyebrows.* Dickens gave her a name a little like that of his mistress, the beautiful, cold goddess of the later books.

The Dutchess announced last week that of all the unpleasant things Dickens did to his wife, the worst was inventing the name Lady Maria Clutterbuck for the author of her cookery book. Clutterbuck. Wife as dunce. He liked to joke about her awkwardness. Why did the Dutchess mention Dickens? Watching to see my response? She must know by now that I have invaded Dutchessville, in my thoughts at least. It takes nothing from her. I have no interest in Victorian domestic life, rather the dark business of murder and obsession.

Fire burning, rain falling.

"You're being silent," the Dutchess said from the kitchen where she was making a medieval stew from meat I would have called inedible.

"No, love," I said, "I'm not being silent. I'm just not saying anything."

A chill autumn night, and the two of us sat on the back porch in wicker chairs, bundled up in winter clothes, long scarves and funny hats, to watch an eclipse of the moon. The next one wouldn't happen until after the beginning of the new millennium, and so we paid tribute to its rarity by staying up late, while inside the fire died and the slow wheeling of the planets brought earth and sun and moon into alignment. The shining sphere of the moon, floating mirror where once, they say, men walked, moved slowly into the shadow of the earth. Such things. We all live in the shadow of the earth.

The Dutchess was whistling under her breath. It had been a quiet day. Neither of us went to town, and in the afternoon we took a long walk on the road that starts at the sawmill and leads on for miles into the woods, first along the millpond and then uphill and down through thick woodland, the air damp and fresh as you travel along the narrow road, wondering who is ahead, who is leading you forward, waiting, wondering where the road will end and whether you want to get lost and sleep cold and helpless in a wet corner of the woods. You hear the soft wind, occasionally the rustle of feet, a squirrel running away over the leaves, a sudden explosion of wings, and silence, you hear silence.

A pile of wood, thin sticks, abandoned on the path ahead, like an altar to the woodland god, the Dutchess said. We walked past and onward to the place where the road ends in a clearing, trees surprisingly large to have escaped logging, thick yellow birch, white birch, spruce, hemlock. We stood there in the clearing, had a piss, turned back, and followed the road to the sawmill, past the metallic glow of the pond, the little waterfall that perhaps once drove the mill, past the old blue truck sinking into the earth, and back home to sit here in the night.

The moon was half covered, and we could feel but not quite see each moment's gradual expansion of the shadow over the shining surface.

"I had a letter from Susan," the Dutchess said. One of the little Dutchesses.

"What did she say?"

"Orland's dying."

"He isn't that old. He's probably just making it up."

"No."

She was silent again.

"I want him to come here," she said.

"Why?"

"So I can be with him."

"You left him."

The shadow was further over the moon, and at the edge of the shadow a pale perfect ring of green light.

"I didn't want to leave him."

"It's what you decided."

"You bullied me."

"You agreed."

"Sometimes I thought it would kill me," she said.

"You screwed around. You sneaked out to come to me."

"That's not the same. I loved him. You never understood that."

Around the vanishing moon, stars and planets, multiple, bright, nameless.

"I want him to come here to die," she said.

"And what do I want?"

"Whatever it is, you'll do it."

"Will I?"

"Aren't you already writing that Drood thing?"

"Only in my head."

"In your head."

I couldn't quite make out the tone of that last remark and wasn't sure I wanted to. I shivered from sitting out in this cold darkness. We waited, and gradually the moon disappeared.

A Monday morning, grey and grim. I wonder, does the Dutchess believe I should have left her there, with Orland? Fucked her and moved on? *Oh Billy Magee Magar.* I could do no such thing. She must know that. Young Meg picked the wrong man for that. It was Monday morning, and I looked at the picture on my desk as I waited for Elaine to come and tell me what to do.

Bobby Shafto's gone to sea. The grey boats out there

in the fog on their way to war, steel against ice and torpedoes. He'll come back and marry me. No, he won't, he won't. Bobby Shafto's getten a bairn. Has indeed getten a bairn and then vanished with the grey ships into the noise of war. I looked at the picture on the desk in front of me as the dim light of the window fell on it, a picture of my pretty mother at nineteen, just before Bobby Shafto came along on a Canadian merchant ship put in at Belfast for repairs, and, with whatever lies and charm and force, got her up the stump in no time at all. He went off promising to come back but was never heard of again. So I was born and she was shamed, and over the years she would claim to be the widow of a heroic sailor who went down with the ship, and maybe so, how else not to have found him later on, unless, like some country maid in a folk song, she never asked his name but only laid her white flesh beneath him in a green field on a bright spring day, as girls have gone to boys forever amen. She was RC, her family from County Wicklow in the south, and the priests were at her to give up the child, but she escaped from the home they put her in and got herself to England and then somehow to Canada, and by then she was, in her own mind, a war widow. She rented a little frame house on Nairn Avenue in Toronto and left me with neighbours while she got on the Rogers Road streetcar and then the St Clair car and down Bay to where she was a clerk at Eaton's.

We were deeply in love, my mother and I, and only in later years did I discover that the headshrinkers called this wrong. She kissed me goodnight and woke me with a kiss in the morning, and every day, before she left for work, she would stand in front of me and spin round, and I would tell her that she looked beautiful. Sometimes when she was away I would play with her makeup, try on her high heels. I loved her so much I wanted to be her. When she came back from work, the same streetcars in reverse order, she would fetch me from the neighbour's. We would come home for tea, and in the evening we would listen to *Lux Radio Theatre* or *Amos 'n' Andy*, and she would explain it all to me. I would go to bed, and she would read *Ladies' Home Journal* — Mrs Elva Burge at work brought it for my mother when she was done with it — and I might wake in the dark and smell the cold cream she put on her face at night and hear her getting into her bed across the room. She called herself Mrs and said that her Canadian sailor husband had gone down with his ship. She loved me best of all, and so far as I was concerned, this was perfect happiness. I liked Mrs Hamp, the neighbour who minded me during the day, but mostly I waited for my mother to come home.

There is always an end to Eden. She married Ray, who had asthma and a hardware store, and there was more money but less love. He was slow and decent, and in spite of his wheezing, he outlived her. I grew hardened to her abandonment of me and of that perfect love and happiness we shared, but I couldn't forget that something had been lost, and when I was grown and found myself among women, I was always searching for the vanished perfection. The doctors would say that I must be ruined, but the doctors are wrong, only I always expected a return to paradise. There were girls who wanted friendship or a little fun, but I wanted a straight train to heaven. I was always disappointed until the adventure of my first adultery, insatiable upon the rich flesh of Orland's naughty wife. It was forbidden, and it was perfect. I swore I couldn't live without her, made her leave him, and now here we were, facing the dark days of the year, and she said she wanted to bring him back. Time foreshortened, and the years that had gone by, second by second, had turned themselves into bits of memory that could be canvassed between sleep and waking, between thought and thought.

Elaine stood by the door looking at me, as if she might have been there unnoticed for a long time.

"Bobby Shafto's gone to sea," I said.

Sometimes she is more tolerant when she thinks me mad.

"Wants to see you," she said. "If you can spare the time." Elaine knows I have been in the company of the absent, led astray by phantasms.

"Who is it?"

"Maude McIsaac."

"Again?"

She nodded.

Maude is a pleasant and well-spoken woman who is a kleptomaniac. The doctors can't do much, it seems, and the courts are losing patience.

"Send her in," I said and prepared to be censorious, though I know it would do no good. We would offer to make restitution. What else is there?

I was walking through the fallen leaves under the bare trees with Jane the Carpenter. The sun was not far above the horizon, and light fell in little patterns of brightness on the forest floor among the underwater greens of spruce and hemlock and fern. The vertical trunks of the trees, grey columns standing apart in the filtered woodland light, led us onward into some ancient story. Jane was telling me about the beauty of wood, how she had laid hands on an old apple tree, milled it herself, and was making small boxes out of the hard, fragrant wood. I had contracted to buy one of her boxes as a present for the Dutchess. Today's outing was planned for all three of us, but the Dutchess had come down with something and lay abed in our room amid the clutter of books and newspapers and clean laundry and dirty laundry, suffering from fever and chills. We had forgotten our plan to walk in the woods with Jane the Carpenter until she arrived at the door, so I made the Dutchess a hot toddy, and she sent the two of us out for our hike. Now Jane and I walked, like Hansel and Gretel, hearing the soft whistle of the wind that moved through bare trees and over fallen leaves, and now and then the rustle of a squirrel or the screech of a jay. See the two figures far off there in the cool golden light. We see them, but we can't quite remember who they are.

"This morning ," I said, "I was sitting out in the sun on the porch with a book. I heard a great clattering in the sky. A helicopter flew by, and I was sure it would come back and land, and a man in uniform would tell me that they had come for the Dutchess, to take her away."

With her short brown hair, pale face, and grey eyes, Jane the Carpenter looked boyish and very young. Wicked uncle takes the innocent lad into the woods and murders him under some mysterious compulsion, but the lad comes back to life and returns in the night to haunt the bad man. The days pass by like years, the years like days, and everything is possible. John Jasper, we must assume, killed his nephew.

"You have such ideas," Jane said.

"Yes," I said.

We walked on, our shoes scuffing the leaves.

"What shall we have for dinner?" I said.

"I won't stay. Mary's too sick to cook."

"I'll make Winter Soup and Roast Something for us all. She'll get up to eat."

Jane said nothing. I took that for agreement, and we followed the old road further into the woods.

"Have you ever read *The Mystery of Edwin Drood*?" I said.

"Who wrote that?"

"Charles Dickens."

"We read something by him in school."

"The Drood book was never finished. He died with half of it written."

She stared at the sky again.

"So you're going to finish it?"

"I wouldn't be the first. Still, it's a temptation."

"What's the story about?"

"A murder. Or at least we assume it's murder. The body isn't found."

We walked on as a cloud blew over the sun. The woods were different, colder. Jane put her hand, long, shapely, though hardened and capable, up to her neck as if to protect herself.

"Maybe it's time to turn back," I said.

"Always never walk forever," she said.

Jane the Carpenter is a mystery. I met her when I defended her on a charge of theft, money missing from a house where she had been building a set of kitchen cupboards. I got the charge dropped at the preliminary hearing. There was, in fact, no real evidence, though it was clear that there was more to the story than had been told by the couple who had laid the charge or by Jane herself. After the case, I hired her to do some carpentry around our house, and both the Dutchess and I found that we liked having her there, quietly working away, pretty in her boyish way. We kept finding new jobs for her to do, adopted her for a bit, though she would disappear for days and then turn up again without explanation. Sometimes she answers her phone, sometimes she doesn't. I tell the Dutchess that Jane the Carpenter has another existence somewhere else in the universe and needs to go there from time to time, and I almost believe it.

The sun was far down the sky by now and casting long shadows across every open space in the woods. The wind blew in gusts among the tall spruces or shook the branches; a solitary brown leaf came loose and fell. The empty spaces between the trunks were full of golden light, but there was an edge of darkness, and everything was growing cold. At the end of the road, the car waited to take us back to a house and a warm fire. The Dutchess would be curled up in bed, waiting for us. Unless the helicopter had come for her. Or perhaps it was waiting to take Jane the Carpenter off to her other life and the Dutchess with her.

Come close to the fire, children, and wicked uncle will stroke his goatish little beard and summon up ghosts. The divine music chases its soft echoes through the spaces of the cathedral, the voice of the lay precentor leading the chanting of the psalms, his voice strong and pure. Yet to the precentor himself it all sounds diabolical. *The echoes of my own voice seem to mock me with my daily drudging round.* He is driven by longing for something more, and the longing has turned murderous. Dickens had lived for years on his own huge reserves of vitality, the certainty that he was right, the energy that was like a kind of possession; he had been in and out of a hundred lives. Bernard Shaw said that *Drood* was the work of a man already three-quarters dead, and there is a mortal intensity about Jasper, a confusion of love and hate.

I stroked my beard (grown when I first came here as a deliberate eccentricity, a defence — look, Mephisto come from away — and by now something I keep because I am used to it), stroked it as I always do in certain moods, as if drawing the hairs to a point would bring concentration to a point as well. I looked into the fire. The flame was calming, as for a hundred generations before me, though fire was a luxury now, inefficient, out of date as a way of heating. I grew up with a furnace turned low. My first fire, the first I remember, was in high school, the graduating class at a final get-together on a beach with a great pile of burning driftwood. Across the fire the faces of the girls were masks of unbearable beauty. Now, like some primordial groaner in his cave, I drew close to the flames, touched the hair on my face to feel myself alive.

The air in the house smelled of the mussels we had eaten for supper, greedily scooping them from their shells. On the way home from work, I picked them up at a mussel farm in a cove near here, driving down the gentle hills between the fields and then looking over the tidal flats to the water. *The nets are unwound; they hang from the rafters over the fresh stowed hay in upland barns.* In the bright summer we dig clams at low tide and taste the salt in their flesh. We live a small, provincial life at the edge of the great sea.

The wind was blowing in vicious gusts as I stood on the pavement outside the bus terminal and watched the men and women get out of the bus, bending themselves away from the rain and sleet, scurrying toward the terminal or gathering in a little hunched group waiting for the driver to pull the cases out from underneath. The lights of the terminal shone on the wet pavement, and the headlights of the bus stared madly into darkness. Winter was upon us, that dire fate. Gather in the longhouse, bodies close together in the fug of smoke and breath, clothed in the skins of animals, eating flesh. Rain blurred my vision as I waited for the man whose wife I had taken away, tried to remember his face.

In front of me, a stocky young woman took off her glasses and rubbed them with her fingers, put them back on and stared about, looking for love. The bus has come from far. In winter. Lovers nested tight together. Lonely night travellers seeking rest. No sign of Orland. The driver threw more suitcases to the wet pavement. Cars passed, lights across the long strings of icy rain. Skins wet, we all watched the world go past. This is the end of the day, so long now. A tall Chinese boy lifted his backpack and walked away into the darkness. Stoics, we endured, waiting. Ice. An old man on crutches was trying to go by me, and I knew he would fall, but he stopped, breathless, and looked at me and spoke my name.

Orland. Pale and wild-eyed. One-legged. The Dutchess didn't tell me that he had only one leg, and I was furious. It made all the difference. What were we to do with a gimp? Dying, she said he was dying, fine, she is a notorious liar when it suits her purpose, and her purpose was to have her old man in the house after twenty years, and the story that he was dying was as good as any. Dying men can't get on the bus. Well known. He was here and struggling to get his breath, and I wanted to kick the crutches out from under him and watch him go down. He closed his eyes. Dying. Bring the old man here to expire. Bury him in a field or feed him to the crows. *Oh Billy Magee Magar.*

"Orland."

He nodded, eyes still closed, breathing heavily. Stertorous, the word for such heaving breath, pant, wheeze.

"Do you have a bag?"

"I lost it somewhere."

No wonder he couldn't keep his wife. Incompetent even in his dying. Now he opened his eyes, and they were watery and red. Was he crying with joy to see the Samaritan who would take him home safe and tuck him up with a white warm belly to comfort him? More likely the rain, sleet, hail, whatever it was coming down on us.

"You've only got one leg," I said.

"Lost it," he said.

Leg, luggage, bits and pieces dropping away into the garbage can, a shedding, ceremonial divestiture by the wise elder before he walks naked into the storm. We have much to learn from the other tribes, and none of it will improve us. A woman was staring at me, murderous. Long nose with a drop of water at the end of it. Tall. I had represented her husband in a rancorous divorce proceeding. An ugly business. No wonder she wanted to kill me. I should have been a priest and grown wise. Orland was staring at me.

"You're fat," he said.

"No," I said, "I'm not."

Get him to the car. That was the next thing to be done, and the heater turned on, two chaps to thaw and hit the road. The Dutchess awaited us, dressed in all her splendour. A woman was tapping on my arm, then tugging.

"Are you from the tourist bureau?" she said.

There was a growth on her chin, and she wore a purple rain suit.

"There is no tourist bureau," I said. "It's closed for the winter. No one comes here in the winter. You should get back on the bus."

She turned, and a young women with a big smile received her into the faith. The freezing rain came down harder, a cold immensity falling upon us from the poisoned skies, and I could feel my trousers growing sodden with it. Orland had closed his eyes again.

"To the car," I said into the wind.

"You don't need to shout. I'm not deaf."

"Wonderful thing, a man of your age. Don't slip on the ice."

I led the way across the parking lot and got him stowed, the crutches in the back seat with the two bottles of Jameson's I'd picked up earlier. Word from home. Note to self: do a little research into the history of Irish whiskey. Once I was myself aboard, I started the engine, turned the heat as high as it would go, and drove out of the parking lot, back end swinging wildly on the ice, not quite killing new arrivals, and off we went toward the end of the world.

That night we lay in bed after Orland was stowed in one of the other bedrooms wearing the Dutchess's nightgown since, bag lost, he had no nightclothes of his own. His heavy breathing was audible through the closed door. The crutches were close to the bed in case he needed to rise in the night, the little case of diabetic equipment which had emerged from the pocket of his coat, saved when all else was lost, on the table beside him. After dinner, he had taken the thick socks and boot off his one remaining foot, which was misshapen, toes missing. The other leg gone altogether. They were cutting him to pieces, starting with the toes. Soon he would be nothing but a talking head. The foot was swollen and had a nasty red spot on the heel, and we soaked it in hot water and Epsom salts, which the Dutchess had on hand, having been warned.

"Well then," I said to the Dutchess, "he's here."

"Do you hate it so very much?"

"Is he really dying?"

"Can't you tell?"

"He could go on like this. Keep trimming away a few bits."

"He has congestive heart failure," she said. "He always had an enlarged heart."

An enlarged heart: Orland had a big heart, true enough. There was the way he welcomed me to their house when the cast had a party while we were rehearsing *The School for Scandal*. Curator of the university museum and art gallery, collector of the folklore of back country Ontario, amateur musician, lovely man whose wife I would steal away. He sat on a straight chair, an old guitar in his hands, and his elegant fingers plucked at the strings and made soft chords while his clear baritone voice sang old songs and taught them to us who sat at his feet. *There were three crows sat on a tree. Oh Billy Magee Magar.* Later in the evening, several beers to the better, we stood in the kitchen, a narrow room with children's bright crayon pictures on the walls, and I was telling him how I'd been born in Belfast and found that I was ready to tell about a poor girl betrayed by a sailor as if it were one more folk song. In the doorway, I saw the young Meg, her hair fastened up on her head in combs, the smooth skin of her neck, a black dress. I made myself look away from her, and I met the gentle brown eyes of her husband, who smiled at me as if he understood how I must be struck by her beauty. I stopped in confusion, said only that I'd come to Canada very young. Orland's big heart. I took the pretty Dutch girl away from a man who was in every way my moral superior. Am I to make it up now, as witness to his deterioration? Wicked uncle learns nursing.

Rain and sleet blew against the window on a gust of wind.

"It's cold out there, Dutchess," I said.

She reached over and put her arms around me, and the two of us clung together for warmth.

"I need to have him here," she said. "I never stopped thinking about him. He was so good with the girls, all those years."

Other lives sat in the darkness watching us.

"There are no other lives," I said to keep them off.

Outside, a few thin flakes of snow were dropping through the empty air, the first of the year, the effect tentative, a hint of what was to come, no wind, only the small white flakes, and in front of the fire Orland lay watching Oprah Winfrey. The television is seldom off since his arrival. He claims that TV is the new folklore, that and tabloids like *The National Enquirer*, and with them he spends his time. No longer driving down back roads asking frisky old fellows what they remember, the stories they heard as children. That's all gone, he says, and what the people are expressing, the new magic stories, are told on *Oprah* or picked up at the supermarket. It's possible that Orland is right. It's also possible that he's dropped one of his oars and the dory is drifting.

This morning when I got up, a heavy dew lay on the grass and fog in the hollows, but as the day went on, the air grew sharper, and now these flakes of snow. A Life Skills day, and I had arrived home before the Dutchess. I had made Orland a cup of tea and brought in more sticks, built up the fire when I saw him shiver.

"I think I could write a chapter about the taboo of embarrassment," Orland said as he watched.

Wicked uncle did not want to discuss deep matters with this dying man. We should be hauling out the hot water and Epsom salts to soak the remaining foot, which swells alarmingly. The Dutchess will do that and feed him his antibiotics when she comes in. I took some chicken stock out of the refrigerator to make Winter Soup, famous for its curative powers. On the way home tonight, the Dutchess plans to stop and buy a portable TV for Orland to have in his room, so he can watch from the bed. In the evening, she goes up and sits there with him, and I don't know what they do or what they talk about, death perhaps, or what it was like when they were together long ago. Perhaps he strokes her round belly with his delicate white hands. I know not.

At the registry office today, I spoke to the Renaissance Girl. She is much the age of her avatar, seventeen or so, but the ermine girl had already been seduced by a Sforza prince and borne a child (her eyes attentive as she holds the ermine in her long fingers, the sharp, dangerous snout of the animal close to her delicate throat, their faces bent the same way). The girl in the Registry Office is dim and polite, yet she will have a history, which is all still to come; the brightness of possibility shines on her exotic face. All future time will one day be a few past facts. She will never know her own beauty. She would have been confused and offended if I had said her face and body were archetypal, her back and arse like stem and flower. So instead I told her about my friend who has the landing field for UFOs — I'd seen him at lunch and asked if he'd found any traces of unobserved use. None, but he lives in hope. The Renaissance Girl was made uneasy by all this, and I forbore. Am not Leonardo, cannot express my hunger for the mystery of her untouched youth. Will smile and pass by from now on. Perhaps I have never grown beyond my young days, when every attractive girl was a promise of the paradise garden, when I expected so much, gladdened by an eyebrow, a nose, a hank of hair, a breast, falling in love twice a day, never satisfied. Only pain could make it right, an obsession with the impossible, tantrums to make it happen, and here we are, the Dutchess knitting up the dropped stitches, comforting her husband's last days.

The television made its noises, and I heard Orland shift on the couch. His body is white, the skin smooth and mostly hairless. The shape of muscles is visible under the skin of shoulders and arms, but the muscles are betrayed by the useless, flopping heart, and any amount of activity exhausts him. Sometimes he watched me intently, and I wondered if he thought we should talk about the past. There was no peace to be made, and when he watched me like that, I wanted to put a pillow over his face and finish him.

John Jasper, if we are to trust the clues, choked his nephew to death with a long black scarf, a detail of clothing that Dickens added in revision. From the beginning, Dickens loved his murderers. The irremediable

Sikes. Old Orlick. There is some indication that Jasper was connected to the Thugs, those philosophic killers, adepts of the goddess of destruction. *All creation is the sport of my mad mother, Kali.* To see that a thing exists is to will its destruction. To know is to annihilate. Orland's flirtation with death provokes a more focused rage. The Dutchess leaves us alone here to tempt me. Even when the three of us are locked in the house, gathered at the fire, it is too silent, too bare to bear.

Wicked uncle seeks his whimsies. The Renaissance Girl is dimwitted, will not know her secret face. I never met my father, never sired a child — a state of winter, even with the sweat of the Dutchess's great things damp on my chest.

The goddess Oprah spoke, her followers roared, and Orland, her student, mumbled something. The dory gone adrift on the great waters.

The storm surrounded the house, and the snow came from all directions, sweeping across the hills and spinning through the empty trees, shaping itself with the pattern of the whirling wind, millions of flakes thick in the air. The light was almost gone. I crouched by the fire and remembered the panting white figure upstairs and wished the Dutchess would return. The way the eyes looked at me from some other world was too difficult, and the growth of whiskers around the mouth, the lips as red as if thickly coated with lipstick, wet as blood.

There was a loud knock on the door. As I went to answer it, I knew that it was someone come for him, someone in authority, men in uniforms who would take him away to die in a sanitary place where no one need observe. When I opened the door, a man stood there, younger and shorter and thinner than I am, straight blonde hair, features that looked as if they might have been carved from wood, a wide smile, his clothes covered with snow as if he had walked a long way through the blizzard. Hanging from his shoulder, a small knapsack.

"Dropped me off at the corner," he said. "It's a good long walk in this kind of a storm."

He was smiling, showing his hard wooden teeth.

"Still, I made it," he said. "I made it."

"Who are you?"

"I'm here to see Orland. I heard he was going soon. I spent what I had on the bus fare and hitched from town, but he left me at the corner and I walked from there. A convivial sort but had to get home to the kiddies."

"But who are you?"

"Jackie," he said. "He was everything to me. I was just a boy."

The wooden features had settled in an expression of senseless happiness. Beyond him, the snow swirled and the night came on. I held the door for him to come in, and he brushed off the snow before stepping over the threshold. Once inside, he took off his shoes, black running shoes with holes in them, holes also in the white socks he wore underneath. A bony toe protruded.

"Would you have a slice of bread and jam that isn't urgently needed by anyone else? I haven't been eating, except someone gave me a sandwich on the bus and a couple of candies. I kept one for later, but it didn't last. You tell yourself that you're not going to chew it, but then you do."

He had taken off the windbreaker he'd been wearing, something with a crest on it, and hung it up on the rack by the door, and now he turned, grinning, and met my eyes. One of his eyes, which were dark green, had an odd mark in the middle of the iris, what looked like a jagged black line extending out from the pupil. It gave his face a tilted, one-sided look. He was cheerful and plausible and I didn't believe anything he said. He had come out of the woods where he had been hiding for a hundred years, waiting to appear in the dark and storm. As we stood there in the hall, the phone rang, but when I answered, there was no one. I heard Orland's voice calling thinly from upstairs. Jackie's head gave an abrupt turn, he stood perfectly still for a second, then picked up his knapsack and ran up the stairs, taking them two at a time.

I went to the kitchen and put on the kettle to make tea, got out a slice of bread, and covered it with butter and dark red raspberry jam. While I waited for the water to boil, I poured a glass of Jameson's and took a little for warmth. The wind sang its plangent ballad in the old kitchen chimney and the kettle groaned. I thought of the Dutchess driving from town in the snow, the road vanishing in blowing whiteness, and half expected her to call and say she'd stay, get a hotel room for the night. To leave me alone with a dying man and this new creature who had come to him. The Dutchess must have invited him. There was no end to what went on without my knowledge. I sipped whiskey and the kettle boiled, and I heated the pot, made tea and poured two cups — sometimes Orland would have a little. It took me a while to find the tray to carry all this upstairs, and when it finally came to light behind the refrigerator, I loaded up and carried it to Orland's room. Jackie was seated on the edge of the bed, holding Orland's hand, while his other hand combed the long thin hair with a small black comb. In the corner of the room, the little TV that the Dutchess had bought for him was playing, a show with a black family and a lot of audience laughter.

"Bread and jam," I said. "And some tea."

"We're getting him all cleaned up," Jackie said. "After tea, I'll get out the razor and give him a bit of a shave."

Orland's eyes were fixed on the TV.

"Families," Orland said. "Families for the orphaned." Then he stopped to get his breath.

"Seesaw Margery Daw," Jackie said, then bent and kissed Orland on the cheek. "Jackie shall have a new master." Orland's mouth hung open a little. The window shook in the wind that was filling the woods with snow, birds, and rabbits in hiding as we all waited for news from outer space. The room was hot, as if Jackie had brought with him some fiery warmth, and there was a flush on Orland's pale cheek. I put the tray on the table beside the bed, and Jackie picked up the bread and jam and ate it with the swift bites of a hungry dog, then drank half the cup of tea. He put down the mug and passed the other one to Orland, placing it gently in his fingers and helping him to lift it to his lips.

I went downstairs. The wind was rising to a howl. Then footsteps on the porch and the Dutchess came in the kitchen door, and with her, like good news, Jane the Carpenter. The Dutchess hung up her coat, and I put my arms around her.

"I was frightened for you," I said. "All that wind and snow."

"Jane was watching out for me."

"It's good to see you here," I said to Jane. I hugged her, too, though it's not my habit, and I noticed as I let her go the darkness under her eyes and how beautiful she is.

"Jane's here to measure Orland," the Dutchess said.

"Measure him? What for?"

"The coffin," Jane said. "I have to order the wood."

She and the Dutchess were smiling at each other as if this was a lovely joke. I put my hand to the glass of Jameson's.

"There's someone here with him," I said.

"Jackie."

"Yes. Do you know him?"

"I knew he was coming. Orland took him in after I'd left. Helped to educate him."

"Where did he find him?"

"The theatre. He's an actor."

"Chicken pie," Jane said.

"Chicken and leek pie," the Dutchess answered.

"We talked all the way out about what we were going to eat when we got here," Jane said.

"Chicken and leek pie," the Dutchess said.

While they cooked, I opened a tin of smoked oysters and sliced up some Cheshire cheese, crushed garlic for dressing. When the pie was almost done, I went back up to Orland's room. Jackie had shaved him and changed him into clean clothes, one of the new outfits the Dutchess had bought him, and he was sitting up in bed as the two of them held hands and stared at the TV. The sound was turned off.

I put a little tray of oysters and cheese and crackers on the table. Frost and snow had gathered in the corners of the window.

"We have chicken pie," I said. "Will you come down?"

Jackie looked at Orland as if he were to decide, but Orland continued to stare at the TV.

"Would it be possible to have a tray?" Jackie said. "The children will eat in their room tonight." He smiled his wooden smile.

"I suppose so," I said.

Jane was the one who took the tray up, and she was a long time coming back down. Hungry, I waited impatiently. The Dutchess stoked the fire and glanced at her mail. Jane was bright eyed when she returned.

"What a pretty boy," she said. Wicked uncle was jealous.

"Is he?" the Dutchess said. "I'll have a look after dinner."

We ate heartily, and the Dutchess and I drank wine. Jane is a teetotaller. When we had eaten, and while I was doing away with the last of the bottle of wine, Jane and the Dutchess vanished upstairs and came back with empty dishes.

"I got his measurements," Jane said.

"You got him to lie down with his hands crossed on his chest and you pulled out your ruler?"

"I have a good eye. Won't be above an inch off either way. I'll leave a bit of extra space."

"Does Orland know about these plans you've got?"

"We've talked about it," the Dutchess said.

Nights when she sat with him, they discussed the making of his coffin.

"What about the girls?"

"They saw him off when he came here. They know."

I sat in a rocking chair and stared into the fire. Outside the house there was a blizzard, and inside we were preparing for death. They were. Myself, I could not approach it with such calm. The deterioration of Orland's body horrified me, and I would have preferred him taken away. Jackie's arrival, his cheerfulness, appalled me. I wondered if he had been Orland's lover. The others were gathered in strange couples, Jackie and Orland, the Dutchess and Jane, and I was left out. I wanted to run away into the snow, but I knew that if I did, I would be lost and not come back, that I would walk among the trees until I found a place to lie down and never get up.

Turning the pages of a book but unable to take it in, I listened while all the arrangements were made. Jackie would stay with Orland, Jane would take the little back room. The fire burned down.

In the night, I woke from a dream about a difficult court case in which I was defending a man charged with plagiarizing from Charles Dickens, who appeared in the court covered by a sheet and intoning the words of the stolen novel. Myself, I was naked under my lawyer's gown and had some difficulty keeping it over my dick, which rose energetically. When I wakened, I heard the wind still blowing. I remembered all the strangers who were in the house, and I was frightened, convinced that a figure was waiting in the dark to do some terrible thing, that Jackie was in Orland's room with a knife. The Dutchess didn't stir as I got up and put on my dressing gown. I stood by the door of Orland's room, listening to his breathing. It was regular enough.

Further along the hall, there was a little light coming from the back room. I wondered if Jane might be awake and reading, and I went down the narrow hall and round the corner. There was a candle on the table by the bed, burnt down almost to the end, and the flame waved and guttered, ready to go out. Fast asleep, cuddled close together in the bed, Jane and Jackie. Her face was younger asleep, but his looked older. They were like two children in a cabin in the woods by candle-light, a bare shoulder, a hand clenched, a breast, nipple like a raspberry for jam, arms twined, their breath so quiet as to be unheard. The candle guttered and went out, and in the dark I made my way back to bed. The

Dutchess turned to me in her sleep and mumbled something.

"Wicked uncle has no more stories," I said.

She mumbled and put her arms around me.

In the morning, the wind had gone down, and everything was white or outlined in white. Bits of snow fell from the twigs and left marks like mysterious tracks going nowhere on the snow beneath. The first up, I watched the sun rise and the snow begin to glitter, and as I put on the kettle for coffee and squeezed oranges for juice, Jane the Carpenter walked into the kitchen, came to me and kissed me on the cheek. Wicked uncle could smell sex, turned to her, and she met my gaze with her accurate shadowed eyes. I thought that she had seen me looking down at the two of them naked in each other's arms.

"Jackie says he heard voices in the house last night," she said.

"Me and the Dutchess?"

"No. Other voices."

"It's an old house, full of old lives."

"I suppose they never leave."

"What were they saying?"

"He couldn't quite make out. The usual story, he said."

"What's that?"

"You'd have to ask him."

I gave her a glass of juice, and she drank it down as I squeezed one for myself. Two lost children stood looking in the window, envious of our warmth and food. The usual story. There were footsteps on the back stairs and the Dutchess came into the kitchen, looked at Jane as if she couldn't remember who she was.

"Eggs," I said. "Will we have eggs?"

"The egg of the universe hatches the world."

It was Jackie speaking from the other doorway of the kitchen. Now we were all in place, but I couldn't tell why we were here. The electric kettle was boiling.

"I'll make coffee," Jane said.

"I'll slice some bread."

"And I'll scramble eggs," the Dutchess said, and opened the refrigerator door.

"Scramble the egg of the universe," I said, "and we'll all shout, 'Chaos is come.'"

Everyone laughed as if I had told a fine joke.

"Is there juice for Orland?" Jackie said. I began to squeeze some, and he wandered to the back window of the kitchen and looked out over the snow.

"Two naked-arse babies run to the woods," he said.

"What?" I said. "Did you see something?"

"Nonsense rhyme."

"Seesaw Margery Daw . . ." I began.

"Sold her bed and lay upon straw," said Jane the Carpenter, in a voice unlike her own. "Was not she a dirty slut, to sell her bed and lie in the dirt?"

"Never heard that one," the Dutchess said.

"That shed," Jackie said. "I saw it last night at the edge of the trees. Watching us."

"I should have knocked it down before now," I said. "Though it's over the property line."

"Leave it to Jackie. Demolition expert. Penny a day to earn my keep."

The Dutchess was cracking brown eggs into a white bowl. She began to whip them, her hand moving in rapid circles. Jackie took the glass of juice I held out to him and disappeared. Jane the Carpenter sat at a chair by the table and watched.

"Is anybody going to town?" she said.

"Both of us, I expect. Work to do even after the blizzard."

"If the roads are ploughed," the Dutchess said. "Will you come or stay here?"

I couldn't help watching Jane's face as she prepared to answer. She saw me watching. Everyone knows everything. I turned away and began cutting bread from a sourdough loaf the Dutchess had baked, beginning it with starter from the pot of fermentation she kept in the basement. Yeast found in Egyptian tombs will still cause dough to rise.

"Stay here," Jane said. "I think there's some wood in the basement I can use for framing. I'll order the rest. They might deliver it by this afternoon."

When Orland tired of TV, she and Jackie could perform for him in ancient postures, the wisdom of the folk embodied in the eternal act. The Dutchess patted my bum as she went to get the frying pan. Outside a jay landed on a branch, and the snow dropped off it. Looking out the window, I had seen this and no one else had except God. Suppose God had not seen it and I fell dead. It would vanish into eternal night. *Drood* would lie unfinished.

Jackie came back with the empty glass, on his face a wide smile as if he had made a great discovery, won the raffle.

"He drank up manfully," he said. Jane was watching him.

"You heard voices in the night," I said.

"I told him," Jane said.

"Couldn't make it out," he said. "But I thought I must know."

"It used to be the doctor's house," I said.

"A repository of old ills. Where else to take your sorrows?"

"It's there or the priest," Jane said. "And the priest will blame you up and down."

"The doctor will nod sagely and give you the mixture as before."

"A World of Old Houses," the Dutchess said. It's the title of a book she's planning.

"I'll drive you to town," I said, "when the eggs are done."

Though it's a Life Skills day, I was afraid that she would invoke the weather, refuse my offer, and say that she would stay with the others to dance around Orland's bier.

"Yes," she said. "I'll get ready after we eat."

Perhaps while all these voices were about I would tell Elaine to report to the world that I was not to be disturbed, and I would invoke the Inimitable there at my office desk. Drood's body was never to be found, only the ring which survived the action of the quick-lime. Outside the house, I heard the loud grinding of a snowplough going past. The roads would be open, but I might have to dig out the car. When I looked to see, the sun was shining across the snow with a blinding brightness that hurt my eyes. I must remember to take dark glasses for driving.

The wind was blowing sleet against the window. I couldn't be sure how it had come about, but here we were, gathered in Orland's room, Jane the Carpenter and Jackie, the Dutchess and I, Orland propped up in his bed with some cushions, his eyes damp and bright, his mouth composed in a smile. I had somehow confessed or boasted to all assembled late at night, in my cups, wanting attention, that I had plans for fragmentary *Drood*, and now, for Orland's entertainment, Jackie and the Dutchess were about to perform a scene that I had extracted from the book, a scene between John Jasper and the pretty young thing, Rosa Bud. Ages were reversed, the Dutchess far too old for her part, but Jackie, who was responsible for all this, cared not.

The storm had gone on for days, and Jane had never gone back to town, though the Dutchess and I had been in and out. When I let out the idea of a Drood play, Jackie leapt on it and insisted there would be a reading. First he said that he and Orland would do a performance together, but Orland would have none of that. His breath was short, his voice thin. It would not do. In fact, I had done nothing about this play I boasted of except brood on it, but challenged, I produced a scene, easily enough stolen from the book. Now Jackie and the Dutchess had pages in their hands, and Jane and I were seated in straight chairs at the end of Orland's bed under the slope of one of the gables, while across the room a chest of drawers served as the sundial against which Jasper leaned, waiting for the sweet young thing to come to him, and another straight chair was the bench where Rosa would take her place. On the wall behind hung an old print of William Lyon Mackenzie King celebrating his first run as prime minister in the twenties, a print I'd found in a junk shop and brought home. All I knew about King was that he was sly as a fox and trafficked with spirits, but he seemed a proper domestic god for at least one room of the house.

I looked toward Orland. The smile was beginning to fade as he grew tired. Jane's face was in profile against the light from the lamp beside his bed, and I could see the tiniest blonde hairs on her upper lip.

"Are we ready?" Jackie said.

The Dutchess, who stood by the door, nodded.

"I think the audience is prepared," I said. "Aren't we, Jane?"

She nodded. She was watching intently, as if the action had already begun. Jackie turned toward the Dutchess, and as he fixed his concentration on her, he appeared to grow taller and heavier, and the wooden features changed. The Dutchess caught his look and shrunk into herself, then walked to the chair and sat down, Rosa Bud waiting for the feared John Jasper to address her.

"I have been waiting for some time to be summoned back to my duty near you," Jackie said, and his voice as Jasper was different, softer, and yet with a hard edge of insinuation.

"Duty, sir?" The Dutchess was too smart to do too much, to fake the voice and presence of a girl, yet one felt her fear.

"The duty of teaching you, serving you as your faithful music-master."

"I have left off that study."

"Not left off, I think. Discontinued. I was told by your guardian that you discontinued it under the shock that we have all felt so acutely. When will you resume?"

"Never, sir."

"Never? You could have done no more if you had loved my dear boy."

"I did love him."

"Yes; but not quite — not quite in the right way, shall I say? Not in the intended and expected way."

The Dutchess, almost without moving, shrank into herself, leaned just an inch away from him, her eyes focused on some distant thing that might give her strength. The two of them were all too good at this. Jackie was a very fine actor. I had not, since *The School for Scandal*, observed the Dutchess's capacities in this line of work.

"Then to be told," Jackie went on, "that you discontinued your study with me was to be politely told that you abandoned it altogether?"

"Yes. The politeness was my guardian's, not mine. I told him that I was resolved to leave off, and that I was determined to stand by my resolution."

"And you still are?" The eyes of the Dutchess had taken on a strange light. It frightened me. She could be anyone.

"I still am, sir. And I beg not to be questioned any more about it. At all events, I will not answer any more; I have that in my power."

"I will not question you any more, since you object to it so much; I will confess —"

"I do not wish to hear you, sir."

In her anger, she stood up and began to move one foot as if to escape, and as she did, Jasper's hand — Jackie's hand was Jasper's hand by now — reached out to touch her, and as she shrank from the touch, the recoil pulled her back into her seat.

"We must sometimes act in opposition to our wishes. You must do so now, or do more harm to others than can ever be set right."

"What harm?"

"Presently, presently. You question me, you see, and

surely that's not fair when you forbid me to question you. Nevertheless I will answer the question presently. Dearest Rosa. Charming Rosa."

Again she rose from her chair, and this time he did touch her, on the shoulder, and a shock went through my nerves. I felt Jane reach out and put her hand on mine, then take it away.

"I do not forget," the man said, "how many windows command a view of us. I will not touch you again; I will come no nearer to you than I am. Sit down, and there will be no mighty wonder in your music-master's leaning idly against a pedestal and speaking with you, remembering all that has happened, and our shares in it. Sit down, my beloved."

He looked at her, and bravely she tried to meet his eyes, but she could not endure the intensity of his glance, the gleam of madness, and she sat. Jasper's obsession drank all the air from the room.

"Rosa, even when my dear boy was affianced to you, I loved you madly; even when I strove to make him more ardently devoted to you, I loved you madly; even when he gave me the picture of your lovely face so carelessly traduced by him, which I feigned to hang always in my sight for his sake, but worshipped in torment for years, I loved you madly; in the distasteful work of the day, in the wakeful misery of the night, girded by sordid realities, or wandering through Paradises and Hells of vision into which I rushed, carrying your image in my arms, I loved you madly. I endured it all in silence. So long as you were his, or so long as I supposed you to be his, I hid my secret loyally. Did I not?"

As he spoke, I could see some kind of strength growing in her, this new young Dutchess, an angry determination.

"You were as false throughout, sir, as you are now. You were false to him daily and hourly. You know that you made my life unhappy by your pursuit of me. You know that you made me afraid to open his generous eyes, and that you forced me, for his own trusting, good, good sake, to keep the truth from him, that you were a bad, bad man."

"How beautiful you are. You are more beautiful in anger than in repose. I don't ask you for your love; give me yourself and your hatred; give me yourself and that pretty rage; give me yourself and that enchanting scorn; it will be enough for me."

The two of them held sheets of paper in their hands and were reading the lines. The lines themselves were tinged with the vaporizing of Victorian melodrama. They had no light or set, only the pudgy face of tricky Willie King above them, yet I was unsurprised by the tears that ran down the Dutchess's face, the low sobbing that began, the struggle to rise and run.

"I told you, you rare charmer, you sweet witch, that you must stay and hear me, or do more harm than can ever be undone. Stay, and I will tell you. Go, and I will do it!"

She stood by her chair, one hand on the back, as if she feared to faint or fall.

"I have made my confession that my love is mad. It is so mad that had the ties between me and my dear lost boy been one silken thread less strong, I might have swept even him from your side when you favoured him."

Her grip on the chair tightened, the grip of the other hand on the pages of script. The low sobbing went on.

"Even him," he repeats. "Yes, even him! Rosa, you see me and you hear me. Judge for yourself whether any other admirer shall love you and live, whose life is in my hand."

"What do you mean, sir?"

I had tried to speed up the next few lines, the plot material about Neville Landless and whether he might be guilty of Drood's death, and I was aware as they spoke that there was something awkward about what I'd done. They seemed almost to lose their way, but then we got back to Jasper's obsession and Jackie's voice strengthened. Outside the window, the wind grew louder, as if in sympathy with his passion. I thought I must find some similar effect to use onstage, though the scene took place at the height of an English summer.

"I am going to show you how madly I love you. More madly now than ever, for I am willing to renounce the second object that has arisen in my life to divide it with you; and henceforth to have no object in existence but you only. Miss Landless has become your bosom friend. You care for her peace of mind?"

"I love her dearly."

"You care for her good name?"

"I have said, sir, I love her dearly."

"I am unconsciously giving offence by questioning again. I simply make statements, therefore, and not put questions. You do care for your bosom friend's good name, and you do care for her peace of mind. Then remove the shadow of the gallows from her, dear one!"

"You dare propose to me to —"

"Darling, I dare propose to you. Stop there. If it be bad to idolize you, I am the worst of men; if it be good, I am the best. My love for you is above all other love, and my truth to you is above all other truth. Let me have hope and favour, and I am a forsworn man for your sake."

The sobbing had thrown Rosa into disorder, and she pushed at her hair with an uncontrolled gesture which was familiar, not Rosa Bud but the Dutchess in some terrible moment that I had seen and forgotten.

"Reckon up nothing at this moment, angel, but the sacrifice that I lay at those dear feet, which I could fall down among the vilest ashes and kiss, and put upon my head as a poor savage might. There is my fidelity to my dear boy after death. Tread upon it! There is the inexpiable offence against my adoration of you. Spurn it! There are my labours in the cause of a just vengeance for six toiling months. Crush them! There is my past and my present wasted life. There is the desolation of my heart and soul. There is my peace; there is my despair. Stamp them into the dust; so that you take me, were it even mortally hating me."

From the other side of the room, I heard a soft moan, and when I looked toward it, I saw Orland with his hands over his mouth like the speak-no-evil monkey, tears running down his face and into his fingers. On our little stage, Rosa began to move away, and Jasper followed.

"Rosa, I am self-repressed again. I am walking calmly beside you to the house. I shall wait for some encouragement and hope. I shall not strike too soon. Give me a sign that you attend to me."

She moved her hand.

"Not a word of this to anyone, or it will bring down

the blow, as certainly as night follows day. Another sign that you attend to me."

The same small, desperate movement.

"I love you, love you, love you. If you were to cast me off now — but you will not — you would never be rid of me. No one should come between us. I would pursue you to the death."

With that speech, the thing was over. Jackie was grinning toward us like a puppet, and Jane began to clap her hands. I looked toward Orland, and he was wiping his face with the small towel he kept by his bed. The tears gone, he gave a couple of little claps.

"What I need to write next," I said, "is the appearance of the ghost of Dickens at the end of the scene. But I'm not sure if he should be the sick old man who wrote that, or if he should, in his ghosthood, have gone back to his bright-eyed youth."

"Why does the ghost of Dickens appear?" Jane said.

"I don't know," I said. "That's just what happens. I can feel him offstage, the Inimitable, a little bored with ghostly life and ready for a performance, a celebration, walking about the room, getting himself ready, taking a glass of champagne, breathing deeply, barely able to wait. After all, he's the only one who knows for sure how it all works out."

"He may not want to tell," the Dutchess said. I was

surprised at her voice, her own now, different from the voice that had spoken those lines.

"I'd forgotten," I said, "what an actress you are."

"I suppose I had too."

"I'd like to turn on the television set," Orland said. "I have to make some notes."

"An't I a clever boy, Orland?" Jackie said. "Aren't you proud of how you trained me up?"

Orland nodded, and we turned on the TV and left him there. Downstairs we had tea by the fire, not saying much, and then found our way back up, Jackie and Jane turning one way, the Dutchess and I the other, to the bedroom we had shared for so long. It all went on well, our life, and yet at times I had the sense that the two of us had betrayed each other — I would never have children, and she would never have peace. Wicked uncle watched lasciviously as she undressed in the half-light of the bedroom, lit by one small lamp with a red shade. Her skin was still perfect, a creamy white, one small mole near the soft indentation of the navel, and though the breasts were heavier now, hung lower, they were shapely, and rich as butter. As I looked at her, I could imagine the voices of children downstairs, her children, playing a game while I prepared to have their mother in her marital bed. It was the end of something when I began to come to her door in mid-afternoon to take her away from her domestic duties, lead her up to the room she shared with Orland, and close the door. I had power over her, I knew, the power of her desire for me, her need for my absurd wild hungers. There were times when I wasn't sure she even liked me. I recognized that I was callow, shallow, hollow, but possessed by a pure fierce lust, and that she couldn't help responding when I told her she was everything I could ever want. She would lock the door of the bedroom, and we would conjugate the verb in all its tenses, and when she was roused and hungry, I would threaten to get up and leave if she wouldn't promise to come away with me. Sometimes a little girl would come to the door, and Meg would steady her voice to say we were having a grownup talk and tell them to eat cookies until she returned to them, soon, soon. But I wouldn't let her come and then go. I tormented her.

Now, in another bedroom, we prepared to be naked together. The endless storm went on over the roof, beating against the walls. Jane the Carpenter was joining her strong slender body to the clever puppet, a whim it might be, or perhaps she was in his power. I imagined that I could hear her bright cries. The nineteenth-century prints of Punch and Judy enacted their ancient violence on the wall beside our bed. We had bought them years ago on a trip to England after we'd seen a puppet show, the old story, one beating the other with a stick, Judy dead, the devil coming for Mr Punch. They lacked Life Skills, Punch and Judy. We saw them somewhere in a park near a zoo, the giraffe watching with us, philosophical and dim.

I went to the Dutchess and put my arms around her, and our heavy flesh was pressed together. We didn't beat each other with sticks.

"My maid Mary, she minds her dairy," I said, "while I go a-hoeing and mowing each morn."

She gave me a little nip on the shoulder.

"You make a fine rosebud," I said.

She drew back from me and looked down at herself.

"Rosebud? Full blown and then some."

"We do eat well."

We tumbled each other into bed and round about the sheets. Slept, and in the darkness I woke and found myself alone in the bed, waited a bit, and no one came. The wind was quiet, but there were a few noises from the furnace. As a way of not thinking about my solitude, I reflected on the long chemical history that made its way here for our comfort, but when my nerves grew imperative, I rose and put on a warm dressing gown and went down the hall. The door of Orland's room was partly open, and I could hear the Dutchess's voice coming from the far corner where he lay in his bed. I couldn't see, but I knew that she was lying there beside him. Her soft voice sounded as if it might be praying or telling some long and intricate tale that wound its way round the facts like a vine round a tree. Turn and turn about: once I had her in Orland's bed, and now he had her in mine.

Along the hall, Jane the Carpenter mumbled in her sleep. I went back to the bedroom, opened the curtains, and saw that the moon had come out between clouds and was shining over the snowy fields.

I woke in the morning to the scream of a power saw ripping through wood. The Dutchess was back in bed beside me, awake, her bright blue eyes staring at the ceiling.

"Jane's hard at work," she said.

"Took a look at Orland and decided she'd better have the coffin ready."

"Yes."

"You don't think he should be in a hospital?" I said.

"He wants to die here."

"Why here? Why not in the house where he lived all those years?"

"He sold that long ago, once the girls were grown up. He's been living in an apartment. A cold sort of place."

"Why?"

"It was all he could afford. They closed the museum and gave him some pitiful pension."

"I thought universities were generous."

"Not if they can avoid it."

I climbed from the warm bed, put on some clothes, and went toward the stairs, observed Jackie sitting in a chair beside Orland's bed, holding his hand and talking to him. The old fellow was certainly getting all the attention a dying man could want. What did a dying man want? Not to be dying best of all, to be dead next best. Not that I knew. Wicked uncle was aware of death only as a rhetorical device. It is a far far better thing I do etcetera.

From the kitchen window, I could see Jane the Carpenter at work, pieces of wood leaning against the wall of the house, others lying on a pair of sawhorses painted pale blue. A noble animal, the sawhorse, infinitely patient, infinitely kind, worthy partner in the dignity of work. It was cold out there. I could see Jane's breath as she worked, wearing an old jacket of mine that usually hung by the back door. It pleased me that she had taken it to guard her against the winter. Adopted daughter, Dickensian sister-in-law, whatever she was, it was good to have her at work out there, and I was pleased to take her a cup of strong coffee when it was made.

Her face had a blank, irritable look when she turned to take the cup. The wind ruffled her hair as I felt it blowing mine.

"You've started early."

"As well start as not. Lying there alone."

I didn't ask the question, only looked it.

"Jackie heard voices in the night and decided that it was his duty to be with Orland from now on."

A maiden betrayed, bereft, and mightily pissed off by the looks of her. I put my arm around her shoulder, but she wasn't having any.

"Not your fault," she said, took a long drink of the hot coffee, put the cup down on the edge of the porch and turned to her work. When I went back in the house, Jackie was standing by the refrigerator door.

"Something for Orland and his little boy," he said.

"Take what you please."

"I met someone in the hall last night, in the dark."

"Not me," I said, "perhaps the Dutchess."

"No," he said. "Someone else. One of the others."

"The others?"

"The old ones."

"John Jasper, I suppose," I said.

"The man who made him be the man. That's what I thought."

"You met Charles Dickens in the back hall."

"That came to mind."

"What did he look like?"

"Hard to see in the dark. He was there as I went to my place at Orland's bed. He had something to say for himself, but I couldn't quite hear."

"The ghost of the Inimitable."

"Who's that?"

"What he called himself sometimes."

"Inimitable."

As he talked, Jackie was pulling things out of the fridge and setting them on the counter, butter, jam, oranges, a lemon, a blue bowl containing the last of a sherry trifle. Outside the saw screamed through wood. Jackie looked toward the noise.

"Last things," he said.

The Dutchess arrived in long skirt and boots with heels, her coat already on, briefcase hanging from her shoulder, hair in a rage.

"I promised to meet with a student before my lecture. Only just remembered." She was pouring coffee into a plastic device used to infuse the drink while she drove the car. When it was full, she turned, waved, and made for the door.

"What do you lecture on today?" I said.

"Piss and shit. Development of the water closet. Next week it's sewers."

She slammed the door behind her. Jackie was piling things on a tray to take upstairs. I poured myself coffee and sliced sourdough bread and sat alone at the table preparing for the day, while outside the house Jane drove nails into wood. Upstairs Orland spun out the threads of his mortality.

Once in town, I closed two property sales, deliberated with a civil servant on the financial consequences of his adulterous fondlings, dictated a letter proposing a settlement for a blind woman who fell in a hole, and, having checked my calendar and found it empty for the afternoon, went and bought Elaine two expensive cigars and left the office in her hands. It was a clear, still day as I drove out from town, a break after the days of storm, and I had an idea.

As I drove up to the house, I saw the half-built coffin leaning against the side wall. It had the old-fashioned shape, tapered at the ends, angling out from head to shoulders and then back in at the feet. Wicked uncle was aware, looking at that old-fashioned shape, how long men and women had been dying in this world, how many had been planted in the soil. Inside the house, I found Jane curled up asleep on the couch, under a blanket and looking like a child. Phantom daughter, unborn sister, untouched lover. I hesitated to wake her, but as I stood looking down, her eyes opened, blinked, and she moved her shoulders to wake herself.

"I hardly slept last night," she said.

"An outing," I said. "I have something to show you."

"I'll be ready in five minutes."

I'd brought mail in from the box when I came. It all seemed to be for the Dutchess from various magazines and universities. Her field, as a collateral branch of

Women's Studies, is a lively one. At the bottom of the pile there was a letter for me, but I looked at the return address and didn't open it. A royalty statement for *The Boy Who Got Everything Wrong*, which still sold an occasional copy but not enough to buy much more than a bottle or two of Jameson's. Note to self: record all the rude verses I recite while driving and make a book of them. Wicked Uncle's Rude Rhymes and Polysyllabic Skullduggeries.

> *A brute I am, I know I am.*
> *I squashed my sister into jam.*
> *I browned my brother into toast.*
> *I frizzled auntie into roast.*
> *I cooked the cat and called it ham.*
> *A brute I am, I know I am.*

Jane appeared, her hair damp at the edges. Water splashed on her face and getting all around.

"Where are we going?" she said.

"You'll see when we get there," I said.

She was wearing her own jacket now, but she helped herself to a large scarf from the rack by the door. It was one of those striped English university affairs; we have never known who left it, but it remains there in case the loser returns to claim it. Jane wrapped it twice round her neck and tucked in the ends, and the two of us set off. The farm fields showed traces of ploughed earth through the drifted snow. Like raked light on a painting, the drifting revealed the uneven pattern of the surface, a texture of dark and light. Sun shone from the west across the tall spruces, which were striped with white. Smoke rose from the chimneys.

We were mostly silent as we drove across the countryside. Once Jane the Carpenter spoke.

"Pounding the peg into the hole," she said. "A children's game."

I could think of nothing acceptable to say in response to that, drove on up and down hills, the evergreens dark against the sweep of snow-covered fields, the brief sun going away from us, and then we came up the final hill and I pulled the car to the side of the road.

"Is this it?"

"Get out and I'll show you."

We walked to the edge of the field. It was broad and flat, and it had been kept mowed so that the grasses and weeds were low bits of stubble penetrating the snow. At each corner of the field was a thick post painted silver, the top shaved to a point.

"What is it?" Jane said.

"A landing place," I said. "For UFOs."

She watched me, not sure whether to laugh.

"He says they're going to come, or have already

come, and he wants a place ready for them to show them that we're friendly."

"Is he serious?"

"There are people with the gift of faith. Millions of Christians are waiting for the Second Coming, and some of them know the exact date."

"Silver rockets at the corners."

"So they know it's for them. In the exact centre of the square made by those silver rockets he's buried a powerful magnet. From far out in the darkness of space, they'll understand that this is a signal, that one man at least is ready to accept them and their holy message."

Jane looked across the field, her head lifted a little, as if the small straight nose searched for some exotic scent coming off the snow and stubble, or as if her eyes, held at a slight angle, could see into the darkness of the woods behind. Now that we have conquered the green world, we no longer fear the darkness of the woods. We look outward into space, inward to the electronic ruins of madness and disease, for the fears that keep us sane. Sex with aliens kills us. If AIDS did not exist, we would have to invent it.

A wind was coming up, and the chill made me shiver. Wicked uncle thought the spacemen wouldn't come for him tonight, turned back toward the car, and on the next hilltop saw the lights of a house where they were not thinking about the silver ships imminent in black distance, only stumbled from pleasure to heartbreak as everyone did in every house. I thought of Orland making dinner in the dark winter evening for two motherless girls. That was one story among all the stories.

> *A brute I am, I know I am*
> *I never gave a tinker's dam.*
> *I cut the tails off all the dogs*
> *And fed a kitten to the hogs.*
> *I sent the baby to Siam.*
> *A brute I am, I know I am.*

Wicked uncle stood by the car door, looked back at Jane the Carpenter, who was staring over the empty field that was an altar to the hope of help. I could almost feel the rise and fall of her breath, and I remembered the naked arm and breast and nipple I had seen in the bed. Coming here was what I could give her, someone else's act of faith. On the way back in the car, we would sing old songs, "My Grandfather's Clock" and other classic tunes, and if she didn't know them, I would teach them to her.

She didn't know them, and when wicked uncle taught them to her, it emerged that she didn't quite sing notes, but she learned the words and followed my lead. The dusk was translated into night, and we followed the track of the headlights over the hills as the wind blew a little snow through the air. Just as we turned the corner that led us slowly up hill to the Doctor's House, I saw a dangerous light in the sky, then the orange dance of flame in the dark air and reflected on the snow. I held hard to the wheel, stepped down on the gas, racing to see my home destroyed, frightened and yet for a moment excited, too, by the power of fate taking charge.

"The house is on fire," I said.

"No," Jane said, "it's not the house. Look, it's back by the edge of the woods."

We were closer now, and as I drove toward the flames, I could see a figure watching them, moving back and forth, arms waving.

"The shed," Jane said. "Jackie's burning down the shed."

I braked the car, and it slid over the snow and gravel at the edge of the road. The two of us scrambled out, tangled in belts, seats, doorways, all the bits of farce that come with rushing, and then I was running across the lawn. Jackie, his face full of laughter in the glow of firelight, was looking toward an upper window of the house and waving. He was so close to the fire that I was surprised his clothes didn't begin to burn, or the wooden limbs under his clothes.

"What are you doing?" I shouted.

"I promised you I'd get rid of the old shed. Remember? Earn my keep. Penny a day. Fireworks for Orland, too. We've got him in his chair in front of the window. Look at the pretty fire, Orland," he shouted. "All for you."

The skin on my face was stinging. I drew away from the fire, which crackled and roared as it ate through the dry old wood.

"You'll set the trees on fire," I said. "The whole woods will go."

"That would be pretty," he said. "Orland would love that. Forest fire, Orland," he shouted.

I didn't see Jane in the leaping firelight, and I couldn't think where she could be. One side of the shed was beginning to collapse, but the back end, closest to the trees, was only just catching. Then it started to roar.

"I put a bit of gas on it," Jackie said. "Gas front and back, to make sure it got a good start."

There was a scrabbling at the end of the shed and in the grass as some animal saved itself. I looked at how close the leaping flames were to the trees, and I knew that the old expression about your heart sinking was no metaphor. I could feel mine dropping away, the strange hollowness that was absolute terror. Jane, her face deep-eyed in the firelight, was standing beside me and holding something out to me. It was the garden hose.

"Use it a minute at a time," she said. "Don't lose the prime on the pump."

She must have gone into the basement to turn on the outside tap and bring the hose. It didn't seem there was time for all that. How long had I been standing here watching? I turned to the fire and pulled the trigger on the nozzle. A fine spray came out and blew back into my face, and I tried again, inept with my growing panic, until I got a long stream of water and directed it at the back of the shed and on the ground and trees nearby.

"Are you putting it out?" Jackie sounded surprised and yet agreeable, ready to change the rules of the game if that's what was required.

"We have to keep it out of the trees," I said. "If the woods go, everything will."

Jane appeared with a garden rake in her hand and went toward the fire.

"Don't go too close."

She ignored me and walked up so close her skin must have been seared. She pushed at the frame of the shed and it bent a little, then she pushed harder, and the front of it went down, a shower of sparks rising into the night toward the trees like evil thoughts. I tried to play the hose on the branches where I thought they might land. I saw Jane turn her head to get her face out of the smoke that had already blackened her skin. She was beginning to cough, and I shouted at her to come away. She moved away from the fire, and Jackie took the rake from her and took her place, walking over embers as if he couldn't be hurt, knocking down the burnt frame, swinging the rake in great arcs. I had stopped spraying to let the pump build up pressure. The parts of the shed that lay on the ground burned more slowly, and I walked closer, my hand over my mouth and nose, and soaked the pieces of framing and the remaining fragments of shingled wall. The back corner was still burning in a high sheet of flame, the gas that Jackie had poured onto it not yet burnt off. I went closer now and shot a spray of water over a wild rose bush that had begun to catch fire. Jane beat her feet up and down on the burning grass. The dance of the end of fire. Jackie worked now to put out the fire with the same enthusiasm with which he'd set it going. He was as frantic as a fly on glass. Wicked uncle coughed and felt mortality rack his bones. Nearby, Jane was coughing. Jackie swung the rake. The back of the shed broke. When he swung again, it came down, and he jumped back as piece of the roof slid toward him, the shingles spitting. I went as close to the heat as I dared and poured water over the ruins. Sizzling and steam. The flame receded a little. When the heat became too painful and I turned away, I saw a figure standing between the fire and the house. It was the Dutchess, and she came no closer, stood silent on the snow as if to observe some lesser species struggle, ants whose hill had been dug up and who scurried in their quaint insect way to save the queen. Above, by the light of a table lamp, I could see a shape that must be Orland propped up in his chair by the window. Close to the fire, my skin was seared, but when I stepped back, I felt my clothes and feet wet, and my whole body began to shake with the cold. We are such small things in the face of fire and ice. Wicked uncle heard himself singing "My Grandfather's Clock" in a loud and unmusical voice, in a rage with the Dutchess because she stood far off like an interested tourist. I had waited for a minute to let the water pressure build up, and now I walked back to the fire and soaked it wherever it still burned. It was small patches burning now, like bonfires, neighbourly and usual, and I thought it might soon be under control, though the heat still came off it fiercely. Jane had found a shovel and was turning over the piles of rubble to reveal the fire beneath, and I turned the hose on the embers, which sent steam into the darkness. There was less flame, and it was growing hard to see what we were doing until suddenly there was brightness all around us. The Dutchess had driven her car over the lawn to play the headlights on the place where the shed had stood. The powerful side lighting made it all stagey, a poorly rehearsed ballet, the three dancers stumbling and bumping against each other. I set down the hose and walked past the burning scraps of wood until I reached the trees, illuminated by the headlights, snow outlining the branches, and I looked for any sign of fire. When I came back, the Dutchess was standing there in one of my old coats with the hose in her hand.

"The worst is over," she said. "You three go in and get warm. I'll watch this. Then we'd better take turns."

At first we all stood dumb and useless, then I turned toward the house and the others followed. Once inside, we looked at each other, blackened skin, eyes reddened from the smoke.

"I'll go up and see Orland," Jackie said. "See if he liked his fireworks."

There was a slash of red across the back of his hand where he'd been burned. I was furious, but I couldn't quite think of what to say. I was beyond speech.

"Do something about your hand," I said.

"Presently," he said and vanished.

"I have no clothes," Jane said.

"I'll get you a dressing gown, and you can wash and dry them." I took off my wet shoes and socks and followed my bare white feet upstairs to find the dressing gown, and when I had given it to Jane, I sent her off to clean herself up and wash her clothes. Wicked uncle poured himself the fireman's medicinal size dram of Jameson's and looked out the window to where the Dutchess stood guard over the remains.

In the morning, the weather had turned warmer. The snow had melted a little and fog stood over the fields and wrapped the trees. Where the shed had been, a pile of blackened boards, a few bits of metal bed frame, an old aluminum pot in the charred ruins. Jackie had promised to haul it all to the road, and the Dutchess would phone Don Maclean, the trucker, to come and take it to the dump. It would vanish, all its old fearful power gone with it. The dolls' heads with their blank smiles melted into flame.

The Dutchess had risen early and made flaky biscuits for breakfast, and now she was in the shower, all hot and soapy, while I poured a cup of coffee and spread rhubarb and strawberry jam. As I turned to the table, I saw Jane the Carpenter in the doorway, dressed in the clothes that she had washed and dried last night while we all sat and waited for the last embers of the fire to go out. Her face was pale and her expression distant. I was sure that while I had slept like the dead, Jackie had come to her bed again, excited by his fire. Pounding the peg into the hole. Or not. We had arranged that I would go to town with the Dutchess, and when Jane was finished the coffin, she would drive my car to town and park it in my space near the office.

I put the biscuit I had prepared for myself on a small plate and handed it to her, poured her a mug of coffee. She sat down at the table. I didn't want her to tell me about the ghosts that Jackie encountered in the darkness, and she was obligingly silent. I jammed a biscuit, poured a mug.

"Charles Dickens could do conjuring tricks," I said.

She met my eyes. Then the Dutchess was in the kitchen, sizzling like a frying pan, warming the air, stirring us up like a bowl of ingredients. She was all dressed in black, pants, boots, blouse, jacket, with a long red bandanna around her neck. It was an outrageous outfit, and I was charmed. Tumbling on the menu for later. Wicked uncle was tweedy, looked not a bit wicked. Note to self: buy a funny hat. Who did look wicked was Jackie as he danced down the back stairs, the black slash in his eye wider and deeper, wooden teeth rapacious, a bandage on his hand. Jane did not look at him. Outside the window, dead sailors waited in the mist. If I sat down at the desk in my office and told John Jasper to speak to me, would he do it?

Note to self: try.

A quiet evening by the fireside. Jane was gone now, and Jackie was upstairs watching television with Orland and writing down the occasional words that Orland mumbled from time to time. The domestic fire burned comfortably, and the aliens were still far off in another universe preparing new diseases. They were the angels who came to earth and tempted the men of Sodom to apocalyptic buggery. Sent out the women first, but the men wouldn't have them; the hole of an angel shines like silver and will teach wisdom to your stiff little putz, and we all long for wisdom. Or do we? Across from me in a rocking chair, the Dutchess turned the pages of her book.

"An old cure for bedbugs," she said. "Beaten egg whites put onto the bed with a feather."

This afternoon, I had sat at a desk with a blank sheet in front of me and, waiting for the ghost of Dickens to speak, imagined that he might materialize through the window beyond which the air was again turning to ice. The handsome figure would walk from one end of the room to the other, the arms striking out with large, theatrical gestures, the eyes flashing.

"It is a perfect mystery," he would say. "There is no solution. Did you think I didn't know that? It was all part of my plan. That's why I left so many and such contradictory clues. Those who think they can find the answer are the greatest fools. The Inimitable hides himself better than that."

It was the wrong ghost. Wicked uncle was not wicked enough to go further. The man who finished Edwin Drood was John Jasper. The other wicked uncle. Finished him with a black scarf. *Basta.* So I stood up from my desk, packed my briefcase, and went to the Registry Office to check title on two properties for clients who wished to buy. A good lawyer always suspects the worst and attends to the unlikeliest of bad possibilities. Hope is for the client alone. In my bag was a colour photocopy of the Leonardo painting. In the middle of my work, I carried it to the Renaissance Girl and put it in her hand, and strange to behold, her face was still and then she smiled. She could see herself there. Wicked uncle left it at that.

When I had finished up my work, I went along the streets toward the desk and the blank sheet of paper. As I walked in the front door of the office, I saw red. A great splash of roses on Elaine's desk with that self-satisfied air that florists' roses always have, cosmetic abundance, the cryogenic look of a movie star after a successful facelift. Behind them, Elaine, smug.

"Well!" I said.

Elaine looked toward me. Cat, canary, etcetera. Said nothing.

"Well?" I said.

"He says he wants to move back in."

"Keith?" Keith was the husband who'd scarpered. "What happened to the cocktail waitress?"

"Moved on to the next table, I suppose. He says he's arriving on Saturday to discuss the situation."

"What are you going to do?"

"We'll go out to dinner, somewhere nice, and we'll have a glass or two of wine and a nice meal, and he'll look at me with that cute boyish smile, and I'll light up a cigar and tell him to go fuck himself."

I looked at Elaine's dark eyes glittering from behind the roses, and I knew she meant it. I left her planning the details of her revenge and went back to the sheet of paper on my desk, thought of a few empty words to get me started. The wrong ghost hovered, saying that beyond death there was no imagining the end of the tale. I sat there until it was time to come home. The cupboard was bare and the poor dog had none.

Across the room the Dutchess was watching me.

"It's all right," she said.

I wondered if she had read my mind.

"What's all right?"

"The Dickens thing that you want to write. Go ahead. You know I just like a fight now and then."

"You brought Orland. To get your own back."

"That was an excuse. I would have brought him anyway."

"Couldn't you have left him with the girls?"

"It would be too hard for them. They have little children."

"So you brought him here by the night bus, like a parcel."

"I had to."

"Yes," I said. "You did."

She looked back to her book.

"I can't write it anyway," I said. "I don't believe in it."

The Dutchess was silent.

"Remember, I told you about a girl in the Registry Office who looked like a Leonardo painting? I took her a copy of it today, and she recognized herself."

"Did you tell her you admired her big bum?"

"No, I didn't," I said. "I'm a respectable man."

She smiled at me with a hint of condescension, and I wanted to pull her hair. In the airtight, a log fell and sparks went up the chimney. Pounding the peg into the hole. Yes, we'd have some of that. I have my dignity to consider.

The house was very quiet as the afternoon wound down. It was snowing again, but the flakes were falling straight to earth and there was no sound. No cars passed. No jays cried out in the woods. Jackie had gone to town with the Dutchess, saying he must get Orland some new tabloids. I felt the house crowded with his abandoned ghosts, the voices he heard, the figures he kept meeting in the night, the old doctor, or the Inimitable himself. This morning Jackie announced to me that they were my ghosts, that I was the one who invoked them, though it was to him they appeared. I wouldn't have any of that, Orland's puppet perceiving what I invoked. He saw them, they were his ghosts. Wicked uncle is a sceptic and knows the silence of silence. When he was a clever boy and perfectly adored in that small house, his sharp sayings noted, smart as Jesus among the doctors, his mother told him that there were no spirits in the air. We had no need of fathers above, of holy ghosts, for we had each other. When she was away, I crawled into the closet among her clothes, eager for the smell of her. Even though later she, lapsed Catholic, unrepentant atheist, went off to Bible Holiness with Ray to keep peace in the house, we had a wink between us to acknowledge our shared disbelief.

The house was too quiet, and I wished for a little wind, traffic, sleet against the window glass. I knew that I should go up and see how Orland was faring, but I didn't want to. The one-legged shape in the bed disturbed me. He made me think of his empty years and how the Dutchess had missed him, the husband of her youth, and had perhaps lain awake night after night when I was deep in the privacy of my dreams and thought about her old man far off. Do you love me? I said to her as we lay in Orland's bed, do you love me? Because if you love me, you must leave him and come away with me. All she wanted was a little innocent adultery, poor thing, a kiss or two, a little wet joy, and now she had this madman on her hands. Come, I said, and come again, and then come away, and at last she did.

I delayed going to Orland as long as I could. I looked in the mirror and thought that I looked more than usual like a goat, long nose, big staring eyes, little beard. Shave. Grow it full. I put on a wicked uncle look, but it didn't make anyone tremble. I didn't suppose the arse of the Renaissance Girl would loosen at the glance of those glaucous eyes, though I cried love me, love me; the Dutchess would respond, but she saw me plain, a dreadful thing. I might soon have to abandon all dignity and start investing in property development schemes to grow rich. When the sperm grew thinner one must have silver and gold to spend. Dear old puns. The Dutchess and I would have beautiful young people to look after us, breakfast in bed, massages, and the like. I turned from the mirror and made my way to the stairs.

Orland lay back against a pillow, his eyes closed,

and at first I thought he was gone, but then a breath heaved the chest up. The red lips wavered as if struggling to shape a word, or perhaps it was only an involuntary shudder. On the bed beside him was a syringe, an empty insulin vial. I stood in the doorway, and his eyes opened for long enough to see me there and then closed again. They had left me here alone with him on purpose. Jackie had gone to find Jane the Carpenter in her small apartment, where she hid from him, to bend her to his will. Or he and the Dutchess had gone off to a dirty motel. They abandoned me with this sick old man, and what was I to do about it, admit that he was a good man and didn't deserve his hard life, crave forgiveness? The question marks accumulate until the full stop puts an end to syntax.

Wicked uncle showed his teeth, but the figure in the bed was immersed in the events that shook his flesh. I walked across the room, took a straight chair, and set it beside the bed. Was not Jackie, wouldn't climb in with him.

"Anything you want, Orland?" I said. It was unconvincing, and he didn't open his eyes. His slender, bony hand twitched a little now and then. In the basement, the coffin that Jane had built waited on sawhorses. The snow fell softly and greenhouse gases ate away at the sky. Orland took another great breath that looked as if it would burst his lungs, then sputtered it out again. Jackie hadn't shaved him today, and bristles stood out from the skin. He still had a full head of hair, the grey stiffness of it unnatural against the pale skin. I could see a pulse in his temple, rapid, uneven.

"Would you like tea?" I said. "A glass of ice water?" I knew he wanted nothing, but I couldn't just sit there much longer. I would run away and leave him.

"There were three crows sat on a tree, Oh Billy Magee Magar," I sang quietly. "Do you remember that one, Orland? You taught it to me, but I find I can't remember all the words. When you have a good day, you could tell me, if you remember them. You taught me that during the play. You had your guitar, and you were sitting in the living room of your house, and everyone was listening, and we sang along with the Billy Magee Magar lines. The Dutchess was called Meg then, wasn't she? That was what you called her." I stopped talking and listened to the silence of the house, hoping that I would hear a door open, that someone would arrive. The only sound was the knocking of the furnace.

"There were three crows sat on a tree, and they were black as black could be. I see crows when I drive into work in the morning, scavenging by the roads. Crows and rats and racoons and cockroaches. They'll survive the greenhouse effect, won't they, Orland? Did you make that up to call her, Meg, or was that her idea? I never asked about that. I just assumed you made it up. I'm babbling, Orland, and maybe you'd like it better if I'd just be quiet. Tell you what, I'll read to you. I'll read to you from your book, all those old stories."

I went down the hall to the back room to find the book. The mattress was bare; after Jane had gone back to town, I stripped the bed, and the sheets were downstairs waiting for someone to have the idea of washing them. Perhaps I'd have that idea later, but one should never do today anything that can be put off till tomorrow. The small book came to hand, and I took it back to Orland's room and began to read. Fill the time until Jackie and the Dutchess got back from town and I could stop being wicked uncle the nurse and find a new hobby. Time passed, and I uttered the words, and no one came. Once he turned his head to me as if he might be about to say something, ask something, but then he turned away and closed his eyes. It was in the middle of the second story that he turned to me again, and now the eyes were unfocused and his hand reached out a little, as if it could help get life and breath into him. I knew that Jackie and the Dutchess wouldn't be in time, that he was going to go as I sat here beside him, the last man he would care to have with him at the moment of death. I stopped reading and put down the book. Dying, I knew nothing about dying. I missed my mother's death, the only one that that counted. It happened while I was arriving on the airplane. Otherwise, death was what you heard about, and you sent flowers. Orland's hand shook a little, and I took hold of it. It was warm, and I pressed my Judas flesh on his, the only human thing available. He was making sounds, and I thought there should be old words. He had been kind to me, the fool, when I invaded his sanctuary. There must be something. Anything, not to go in silence. A doctor told me once that right to the last they can still hear. Make a noise, any noise, and now I was singing, "Bobby Shafto" of all things, and out loud, whether for Orland or to shut out the sounds of his dying I couldn't say.

I sang, not looking, and then I realized that the grip of his hand was loose, and when I dared to see him, the face was empty. The UFO had come silently, perfectly, down into the snowy field and had taken him on board. I put his hand on the bed and, not knowing what to do next, did what I'd seen in the old movies. I pulled the sheet over his face. That looked ridiculous, a final indignity, so I folded it back again. I could go to the basement and get the coffin and have him set up in it before they got back, but I didn't think I would.

Come close to the fire, little children, and wicked uncle will tell you things. Such things. I was walking through the autumn woods with Jane the Carpenter. The leaves were falling from a big maple, and as they fell, they rattled against the still-hanging yellow leaves below them, loud in the quiet of the woods. Earlier we had heard geese overhead. The sky over the tops of the trees was clear, with only an occasional streak of cloud. The air was damp and the light clear and the edges of everything sharp, and we had walked a long way into the woods and now were almost back to the mill where we'd left the car. On the lawns of the houses, there were circles of leaves under all the trees, a carpet of yellow or brown that would later be raked up or blown away, but now they made a perfect pattern. A jay cried out, and we emerged from the woods, got into the car without speaking, and drove back to the house.

The Dutchess was sitting at the kitchen table. She appeared to have been ripping the weekend paper apart, and pieces of it lay on the floor all around her. There was flour on her face. Jane looked toward her with some anxiety; we'd been gone longer than planned.

"He just woke up," the Dutchess said. "But I thought I'd wait and see if he went off again."

He. Jane's baby son. It was wicked uncle she first told about her state, came to the office one chill day last March, long after Orland had been washed and wrapped and shipped to the bonfire place and the long winter had turned us white and stilled the water. She came in and found me studying how to respond on behalf of a client being sued for damages after his goat had bitten someone, sat herself down in the client's chair and announced that she was in the family way. Not that phrase, surely, though that's how I've chosen to remember it. Wicked uncle, I'm in the family way. Bobby Shafto's getten a bairn. I wondered for a moment if she wanted me to commence legal action against the putative *père*, but that was a professional deformation, of course, she only wanted to talk. To wicked uncle. I was as flattered as could be and tried to be sensitive and understanding, though that's against the grain and gives me a toothache. Gave it up soon enough and asked who'd put the bun in the oven, as if I couldn't guess, and it was as you'd expect. As I listened to her, a few words, long pauses, it became clear she was planning to keep the little thing. That she had no intention of chasing down Bobby Shafto and putting the bairn in his arms, was prepared to be what's now called a single mother. It isn't all to the bad, the way the world has changed so that Jane wouldn't ever be shamed by it all. Take the bun into the business. Jane and Family, Carpenters. As I listened, I thought this was the time for it and told her the story of my mother and the dead sailor, and we both had a tear in the corner of the eye; old tales retold will do that.

Over dinner at a local eatery we told the Dutchess,

who was eager to exhibit her Life Skills in finding out young Jackie, but Jane said nix, better he didn't know. Bobby Shafto's gone to sea, so long Bobby. It was over dinner that Jane announced she wanted wicked uncle to be the Godfather. Just like Marlon Brando in the movies, I thought: such things. It then appeared that Jane was known to slip off to evensong at Saint Whatsits from time to time and she meant the real show, in church, the bun properly baked and basted while wicked uncle stood by and made wild promises. Nothing for it but to agree. After all, my lovely mother had gone off to Bible Holiness to give Ray a little peace, had a Bible Holiness funeral, a bit long on noise and sincerity for my taste, but what's to be done? And the promises would never stand up in a court of law.

And so, in the fullness of time, a boy child was born, wicked uncle hanging about the hospital until the sharp-eyed nurses were convinced that I had sown the seed. Though it was a long business, it all came to an end with a few stitches, and the Dutchess swept the whole boiling off to our house for the first couple of weeks. The thing was small and red and pooped satisfactorily, a fine thing in babies, I'm told, and I was being taught how to keep its head from falling off when carrying it about. Knowing the world for what it is, I had started a trust fund.

I'd noticed as we came into the house after our

walk in the woods that the sun was sinking and the air getting a nip, so I lit a fire while Jane went off to get the bun and attend to his diaper. The fire was just beginning to roar when she brought him back in, sat herself down on the couch and hauled out a once-small breast with a nipple like a ripe raspberry, and the baby flailed an arm and twitched and gaped and got the raspberry in his mouth and contentedly stoked up on raspberry jam. I put the screen in front of the fire and went out to the kitchen, where the Dutchess was throwing flour and pounding things until they gave in, and out the side window, I saw the golden glitter of late sunlight falling through leaves and branches. Soon the snow would come again. We waited for Orland's ghost, but it did not arrive, unless to her while I slept.

"Dutchess," I said. "There were three crows sat on a tree."

"Oh Billy Magee Magar," she said.

Judy Gaudet

Close to the Fire is David Helwig's fifteenth book of fiction. He has also written many non-fiction books, including poetry, documentary, translation, and, most recently, *The Child of Someone*, a memoir. A frequent contributor to the *Montreal Gazette*, *The Toronto Star*, *The Globe and Mail*, *Books in Canada*, and other newspapers and magazines, he is a founder and long-time editor of *Best Canadian Stories*. After living in Kingston for many years, David Helwig moved to Prince Edward Island in 1996.